PIPER DAVENPORT

Road To
REDEMPTION

DOGS OF FIRE BOOK #2

DOGS OF FIRE

Cover Art
Jackson Jackson

Cover Models
Stock Images

ISBN-13: 978-1-962938-01-3

ONE

Payton

I STOOD STARING at the copious amounts of wine choices in the downtown Portland Safeway store. My best friend Macey and I had been invited to a Dogs of Fire compound get together tonight by Danielle Carver who was a relatively new friend and married to one of the officers in the club.

Funnily enough, she was a kindergarten teacher in the same school district I worked for. Different enough schools where we hadn't run into each other, but we had quite a bit in common and I loved our occasional 'solve the problems of the world' conversations in regard to children.

Her husband was not at all who you'd expect Dani to be married to, but when you met him, you also weren't surprised. Austin 'Booker' Carver was gorgeous, sweet, and wholly de-voted to his wife. She'd been kidnapped a few months ago, and he'd rained down hell on the people who did it and I liked that.

Macey had a man like that and my sister-in-law had my brother, who was totally a man like that, so I figured there was hope for me somewhere in the world. If it started with meeting a few sexy bikers, I wasn't going to complain.

"Daddy!"

I was pulled from my thoughts by the sound of a little girl's voice and thought nothing of it until she appeared at the end of the wine aisle, her blonde hair pulled into uneven pigtails and tears streaming down her face.

"Daddy!" she called out, sobbing.

I rushed to her immediately, dropping my basket and purse as I knelt in front of her. "Hi, sweetie. Did you lose your dad?"

She nodded, her lower lip out in a cute but pathetic little pout.

"What's your daddy's name?" I asked.

"Daddy."

I forced myself not to giggle, because this little girl was unbelievably adorable, from her leather vest with pink flowers on it, right down to her little motorcycle boots. "Okay. What's your name?"

"Wiwy."

"Lily?" At her nod, I smiled. "That's such a pretty name."

"Fank you."

"Okay, honey, let's see if we can find your daddy." I grabbed my purse, left the basket where it lay, and stood. Lily slipped her tiny little hand in mine like she'd known me forever, and we started to walk the aisles.

It wasn't long before I heard a deep voice calling her name, so we followed the sound. We turned down the coffee aisle and Lily tugged her hand out of mine and made a run for the best looking man I'd ever seen.

Seriously. *Ever*.

Tall and muscular with sandy blond hair and a handlebar moustache that rivaled Sam Elliott's in pretty much every movie he'd ever made…except Roadhouse where he had more of a beard, but still the handlebar moustache is imprinted on those of us who love him, so you still saw that moustache even when it wasn't really there. Yeah, he was sexy like that.

"Daddy!"

The man faced her and after a fleeting look of frustration and anger, his face melted into one of unconditional love as he bent down and scooped her into his arms. "Lily! I told you *not* to run off like that."

She wrapped her tiny arms around his neck and kissed his cheek. "I sowwy daddy."

Holy cow, this little girl knew how to work her cuteness. I was transfixed momentarily and turned to walk away when he caught my eye.

"You found her?" he asked.

I smiled. "She found me, actually."

"Yeah, she does that." He gave his daughter a squeeze and then offered me a slow smile. "Thanks for helping her."

My heart raced and I was sure my panties were fighting to stay on as I nodded. "No problem. Okay, well, I should go."

"'Bye, babe," he said, his voice low and sexy.

"'Bye," I squeaked, and continued to stand there.

He chuckled and it brought me back to my body. "You got somewhere to be?" he asked.

I didn't answer. Just turned on my heel and made a rush for the wine aisle again, deciding I'd bring one to the party and buy another six to try to forget my inability to form a coherent sentence.

Never…and I mean, *never*…had this happened to me. Not even when public speaking. I was a teacher and used to addressing crowds. People, no matter their age, didn't scare me. I liked people. They fascinated me. It's why I chose teaching. Impacting the lives of young people while watching them grow into useful members of society made me feel happy and fulfilled. It gave me purpose, and I believe it had given me a confidence no other job could have. I also had parents, not to mention siblings, who loved me. Nurtured me. Teased me mercilessly, but had my back and protected me always. Especially my brother, Brock.

But in that moment, none of my training or love or confidence was of any use. In a matter of seconds, I'd turned into a blithering idiot because of a man. Gah! I couldn't hate myself more if I'd stripped naked and offered myself to him in the middle of the store.

Grabbing the wine, I hightailed it out of the store and into my car as fast as I could. I was comforted by the fact that since I didn't live here, ergo didn't typically shop at the Safeway in downtown Portland, it meant there was little to no chance of running into him again, and I was grateful for small mercies.

Macey and I used to be roommates, but I moved out just before she married Dallas. Coincidentally, Dani and Booker lived in the same building, so we would all be going to the club together. I'd known Booker insomuch as we knew each other's names and chatted while getting the mail, but until he'd met and married Dani, I'd never really had a conversation with him. All I knew was that he was the hot guy in 8C.

After I'd moved out of the apartment, I moved back to Vancouver to live with my parents. It was supposed to be temporary, but I kind of liked coming home to my parents every night. Sometimes Mom even had dinner waiting. Sure as hell beat living in an apartment all by myself with no one but the walls to talk to, and as long as I followed the house rules (which were pretty nonexistent now that I was an adult) and texted regularly so Mom knew I wasn't dead on the side of the road kind of thing, it was an ideal situation. Especially since they charged me a ridiculously low amount of rent and I essentially had the basement to myself, provided I save. So I did. A lot. Who knew having no overhead meant I could save over a grand a month?

Arriving at my old building, I used Macey's code to the

parking garage and slid into her extra space. Dallas was an FBI agent, along with my brother, and they were on an all-nighter, so we were going to the party and then I was going to stay at her place.

Grabbing the wine, I rode the elevator to the lobby and checked in with the guard before being given clearance to head on up to my old place. One of the best things about the building is the safety…and the million-dollar view of the water. Oh, how I missed that view.

I had a key to the apartment but it was for emergencies, so I rang the doorbell and waited for Macey to answer. My phone buzzed and I glanced down to see a text from her.

Macey: Use your key

I rolled my eyes and dug my keys out and let myself in. "Hey," I called.

"Bedroom," Macey called back.

I locked up, set everything on the sofa, and headed to the master bedroom where I found Macey standing in front of the mirror wearing jeans and a bra and holding a shirt to her chest. "What do you think?"

"What are you going for?" I asked.

She turned to me and shrugged. "I'm married to a badass law man, so I'm taken and you better not mess with me or my man will fuck you up?"

Macey could only be described as stunning. Long auburn hair, light blue eyes, and a body to die for, she was sweet and caring as well as beautiful. Her career as a nurse provid-ed a flexible schedule for the most part, which is why she was able to join me tonight.

I laughed. "I take it Dallas said something similar before he left?"

Macey sighed. "Pretty much."

"I think you should wear your Jason Maxx T-shirt. Then no one will bug you."

She chuckled. "Bikers don't listen to country?"

"I have no freakin' clue, but I'd venture a guess if they did, they sure as hell wouldn't listen to *him*."

"I don't know why I'm even making an effort. I'm happy to stay home with wine and a movie."

"But I need my wingman tonight." I grinned. "What did Dallas say on the subject?"

"A *lot*," she said. "But he likes Booker and I guess they had a conversation about making sure everyone knew I was off-limits."

"He didn't!"

"Ohmigod, he so did." Macey opened a dresser drawer and pulled out her Jason Maxx T-shirt, pulling it over her head. "He also said something about me texting him every thirty minutes with an update of how I was."

"He's ridiculous."

"Unbelievably," she agreed with a grin. "Which is why—" Before she could finish her thought her phone pealed and she glanced at the screen. "Speak of the devil. Hi, baby." She smiled at me. "Yep, she's here. We're meeting Dani in twenty minutes. Uh…yeah. Sure. Dallas, *no*. You're an idiot. I love you, but you're an idiot." Macey gave me her 'I might kill him' look and took a deep breath. "Honey, I'll be with Payton, Dani, *and* Booker. I'll be fine. No. No, baby. Every thirty minutes is unrealistic. Well, then you text *me* every thirty minutes and let me know you're okay, and I'll respond," she snapped. "Why yes you *are* kind of pissing me off, Mr. Stone." She turned away from me, but not before I caught her blush.

I left her to her conversation and headed to the kitchen. Opening the fridge I grabbed a pop and sipped, my thoughts turning to the hottie in the store. Silly, but for whatever reason, I couldn't get him off my mind.

"Sorry, Pay." Macey dragged me from my thoughts as she strolled into the kitchen.

I smiled. "No worries. All good with Dallas?"

"Yes." She chuckled. "But he's still ridiculous. I see you

grabbed wine. Did you stop at Freddie's?"

I shook my head. "No, I went to Safeway down here."

"And?"

"And what?"

Macey grinned. "I feel like you're holding back."

I sighed. "I just kind of met the hottest guy on the planet."

"Shut up." She sat at one of the bar stools. "Tell me… details, missy. None of your vague, two-word answers."

"Don't get too excited, Mace. He's obviously married. His little girl got lost in the store and I helped her find him." I groaned. "Why are all the good ones taken?"

Macey wrinkled her nose. "Oooh, sorry, buddy. That sucks."

"Totally sucks."

"Well, maybe you'll meet someone better tonight."

"I'm not sure skuzzy biker guy's my thing, Mace. But maybe I can find someone to get a little freaky with."

"Ohmigod, Payton. Don't say that out loud tonight!"

I grinned. "Why can't I just have fun once? One time, Mace."

She raised her hands in surrender. "Honey, if you want to make a quick change on who you are and have a one night stand, go for it. I will even hold you while you cry because you're not a whore and your attempt to be one, just once, didn't work out."

I let out a dramatic sigh. "I wish I had absolutely no morals whatsoever."

"Says the woman who made Brendon wait six months just to cop a feel."

She had me there. "Well, one day maybe I'll find a guy that believes the same things I do, but I highly doubt it'll be at a motorcycle club get-together."

Macey smiled. "Yeah, you're probably right."

The doorbell rang and Macey checked the peephole before pulling open the door to Dani who looked adorable in her classy biker look. She wore dark jeans, knee-high motor-cycle boots and a tight T-shirt with a Harley and their logo across the bust.

"Hey," Macey said. "I thought we were meeting you."

Dani nodded and hugged her. "Austin got stuck at the club and I'm hoping I can grab a ride with you so he doesn't have to drive all the way back to get me."

I grinned as Macey closed the door. "The more the merrier," I said. "I'll drive."

"Awesome. Thanks," Dani said, and pulled out her phone. She sent a quick text and then slipped her phone back in her pocket.

"We're ready," Macey said. "Should we go now or wait and be fashionably late?"

Dani chuckled. "Now works. People arrive at all hours, but I'm pretty sure most of the crew is already there."

I grabbed my keys and purse and we headed down to the garage and, with the stereo blasting, made our way to the compound.

TWO

Payton

UNDER DANI'S DIRECTION, I pulled into the hidden entrance of Big Ernie's Body Shop at the back, up to the sky high double gates, where she leaned out of the backseat window and entered a code into a keypad before the gates allowed us entry.

"This is only the third or fourth time I've come this way," Dani admitted.

"Oh?" I asked. "How do you normally get in?"

"The front, like normal people." She chuckled. "But Austin won't let me go that way without him anymore. Says it's safer to come this way for whatever reason."

"I can't imagine many folks know this way even exists," I said, and pulled into a parking lot filled with trucks and bikes.

"Probably not. It's only for the super secret members," Dani said, and laughed again. "I'm just waiting to see if they have a handshake I'm going to have to learn."

"Maybe we should make our own up and make them learn it," Macey retorted.

"Chest bump included?" I asked.

"And risk every man in the place getting a hard-on," Dani said. "Probably want to skip the chest bump."

We dissolved into giggles as I parked my car and we piled out. Dani led us toward the large brick building, but before we reached it, the back door opened and Booker strolled out, reaching us and pulling Dani in for an intimate and passionate kiss. I had to look away or I was sure I'd combust…or need a few minutes alone with my battery operated boyfriend.

"Hey baby," he said.

She chuckled. "Hey yourself. I take it you've been watching the monitors?"

He raised an eyebrow. "That would border on stalking, baby. I would never do that."

"Hmm-mm, sure." She grinned up at him. "Have you told everyone to be on their best behavior?"

Booker smiled at me and Macey. "You ladies are safe in our presence. The bathroom has even been scrubbed by a particularly eager club who—"

"*Austin*," Dani warned.

"Sorry," he said. "Young woman."

I laughed. "Wow, the red-carpet treatment. I like it."

"Come on in and get out of the cold."

Booker hung back so we could walk in ahead of him and I followed Dani and Macey inside. We walked through a professional kitchen that was well-equipped with the biggest appliances I'd ever seen…the fridge alone could probably hold enough food to feed a hundred people for a month. We dropped off the wine with a few of the women inside and, after quick introductions, Dani started the tour.

We entered a large common room already packed with biker men and women. The space was filled with sofas, over-stuffed chairs, a pool table, large flat-screen television, several smaller tables that children gathered around for board games, and three outdoor picnic tables, where people were already sitting down and eating.

"Dani, Dani, Dani!" a little girl squealed and ran to Dani who scooped her up and gave her a hug. The little girl wrapped her arms around her neck and squeezed.

I was momentarily stunned as I recognized the little girl, but it wasn't until I saw the man walking towards us that my breath left my body. I blindly reached for Macey who was standing slightly behind me.

"You okay, Pay?" She grasped my hand, even as I continued to stare at the man from the supermarket.

The man's slow smile as he reached us had me squeezing my legs together. "Hey."

He wore jeans that were obviously made for him, a long-sleeved black thermal shirt and a leather vest with several patches on it. He was delicious.

I swallowed, nodded, and forced a smile. "Hi," I squeaked.

"You know Hawk?" Dani asked as she set Lily back on her feet.

I shook my head. "Uh…no, not really."

"Lily found her in the store," he explained as he continued to study me. "And she kindly found me."

Dani chuckled. "You might want to consider a leash."

"A fuckin' short one," Hawk retorted.

I held my hand out. "I'm Payton."

He took my hand and gave it a squeeze. "Hawk."

Lily patted my leg and I glanced down at her as I pulled my hand from Hawk's.

"You were in the stowa," she said.

I smiled and hunkered down in front of her. "I *was* at the store."

"You're so pwetty."

I chuckled. "Thank you, sweetie. So are you."

"Daddy thinks you pwetty too."

"Lily," he said with a groan.

I smiled. "I'm sure he thinks your mom is too."

She frowned. "I don't have a mommy."

"Okay, trouble, it's time you go play with your friends," Hawk said, and picked her up, heading toward the kitchen.

"For the record," Dani said after he was out of earshot. "Hawk's totally single. And his real name's Alex James."

Alex. Sexy. It suited him. For whatever reason, I had a hard time wrapping my mind around 'Hawk.' Alex seemed more fitting somehow.

"Babe," Booker warned. "Don't."

"You are not the boss of me, Austin Carver," she said, and patted his cheek with her hand.

"Fuck me," he said.

"Later," she promised, and focused back on me. "You let me know if you want me to set anything up."

"Um, no," I stressed. "No interference from anyone, thank you very much."

"Got it, babe?" Booker asked.

"I got it, honey," Dani said, and then smiled back at me. "But you let me know if you change your mind."

"I won't."

She winked. "We'll see."

I rolled my eyes. "I could do with some wine. Anyone else?" Macey squeezed my hand and I released my hold on her. "Sorry."

"I didn't need that hand, hon. It's all good." She chuckled and pulled me to a stop. "So that's the guy?"

I nodded.

"He's apparently single."

I nodded again.

"And super, super hot."

I bit my lip *and* nodded. Macey grinned. "I'm all about Payton…remember that."

I let out the breath I didn't realize I'd been holding.

"Thank you."

* * *

Hawk

I settled Lily in the playroom and nodded to Ellie who was watching the kids along with another young club whore…I didn't know her name. Didn't really care to. All I knew was she was good with kids. I stepped out and almost ran into Booker. "What?"

"She's not a whore."

I scowled. "I know she's not a whore."

Booker crossed his arms. "Probably isn't into your warped kind of sex either."

"Fuck off, Booker."

"Her brother's FBI, her best friend's husband is FBI." He raised an eyebrow. "She's protected."

"Fuck. *Off.*"

Booker smirked. "Just so we're clear."

I scowled again. "Fuck you."

Booker nodded. "We're clear."

He walked away, and I stood in the hallway for a few minutes in an effort to stamp down my irritation. The truth was, Booker had picked up on something I wasn't ready to admit just yet. This woman… Payton… fuck, gorgeous name to go right along with the gorgeous woman… she was under my skin. Two encounters and the woman was already under my fuckin' skin.

Fuck!

I dragged my hands through my hair and walked back toward the common room. As I passed through the kitchen, one of the newer hangers on, Laurel I believed, gave me an open smile. "Hey, Hawk."

"Hey, babe," I said.

"You wanna have a little fun?" she purred, laying her hand on my arm.

I forced my irritation down again. For the first time in

years, I wasn't interested in a little fun. At least, in a little fun with anyone but Payton. Fuck!

I smiled and pulled my arm away. "Not tonight, babe, yeah?"

Laurel appeared crestfallen. "You let me know if you change your mind."

I nodded and joined the rest of the group.

* * *

Payton

I stood with Macey, Dani, and a couple of other women, and surreptitiously watched Alex out of the corner of my eye. Good lord, the man was pretty…and popular. A particularly skanky woman was draped all over him and it was all I could do not to punch her in the throat. I bit my lip. What the hell was wrong with me? I didn't know this man. Didn't have any rights to him.

"Pay?" Macey squeezed my arm. "You okay?"

"Hmm?"

"You okay?"

"Oh…ah, yep." I nodded. "I'm good."

She studied me before giving me her 'we'll talk later' look. I formed what I hoped was a sincere smile and focused back on the conversation at hand. I couldn't focus for long, as Alex walked toward us, his face impassive, but his eyes alit with something I couldn't pinpoint. But it was sexy as hell, possessive beyond comprehension, and I felt it all the way through me.

I licked my lips and Alex gave me a slow smile.

Damn it! I must look away. I must look away.

I didn't look away.

As he walked past us, he gently took my arm and, like a rat to the Pied Piper, I followed him. Macey watched us leave, but thankfully, she didn't object.

Alex led me outside, his hand still grasping my arm, before pushing me up against the brick of the building and covering my mouth with his. I was so unprepared for the gentleness of the assault, I dropped my wine in an effort to grab his waist to stay upright.

As his tongue slipped inside my mouth, I sighed, leaning against his hand on my cheek. God the man could kiss!

His other hand was at my waist and holding me against him, but when it slid up to my breast, it brought me to my senses and I pushed against his chest and broke the kiss. "Alex. Don't."

"Fuck me," he whispered, and dropped his forehead to mine. "I thought this would work."

"What?"

"Kissing you."

I frowned. "I don't understand."

"I know," he said, his arm wrapping around my back. "I thought I'd get you out of my head, but I just want more."

He kissed me again, but this time I was prepared and forced my mouth away from his. "We can't do this."

"Why the fuck not?" he challenged, his face inches from mine.

"Um, gee, I don't know. Maybe because we don't know each other."

"Babe, you're fuckin' hot and I know you think I am, so what the hell's stopping you?"

I took a deep breath and fought back a few choice swear words. "Please let me go."

"What the fuck?"

I shoved at his chest again. "You heard me. I'd like to go back inside."

"Babe, don't play hard to get."

I gasped. "Oh my *god*, Alex, I'm *not* playing hard to get. I really *am* hard to get. Let me go!"

He released me immediately and stepped back. I turned to go, but he caught my arm again. "This isn't over Payton."

"I beg to differ."

He chuckled. "You call me Alex, you kiss me like that, *and* you look the way you do? Babe, I'm puttin' you on notice. This isn't fuckin' over."

I couldn't stop the shiver that ran up my spine, but I squared my shoulders and pulled away from his touch. "And I'm putting you on notice, Alex James. I'm not some whore that will melt at the sight of your pretty face, or the sound of your sexy voice. I own my own mind and I don't fold easily. I'm also unlisted and I know for a fact, there isn't anyone in that room currently who either knows where I live, or would tell you. So good luck with your pursuits, sir, but you're going to get nowhere pretty damn fast."

He laughed.

Laughed!

"Fuck me, you're hot," he said, and pushed me against the wall again.

"What are you doing *now*?" I demanded, and yet, I went with it. I couldn't seem to help myself. I wanted him to possess me…so much for having my own mind.

He grinned. "I need to explain somethin' to you, baby. You challenging me only makes me want you more—"

"Well, I have no intention of *not* challenging you, so it looks like we might be at an impasse."

"Shit, an impasse." His grin widened. "That's just gonna make this all the more fun."

I blinked. "I'm afraid you're going to be stuck playing with yourself on this one."

He cupped my cheek, his thumb brushing along my jaw. "Gorgeous and funny. Baby, you're just puttin' the nail in your own coffin."

"Lovely," I retorted. "You're planning on burying me?"

"The only thing I plan to bury is me inside you, so wrap your mind around that, Payton. You need a day to come to terms with that fact, then, I'll give you the day. But I always get what I want."

"As romantic and appealing as that sounds, handsome,

you're barking up the wrong tree. But you feel free to fantasize all you want. Day after tomorrow when you still can't find me, you'll figure it out."

Alex lifted my chin, his smile softening from leering to sweet and sexy.

Well, crap!

"When I find you tomorrow, baby, you and I are going to have a very intense conversation before I share those fantasies with you. And as far as hard to get, I'll be hard when I get you, but you'll enjoy every minute of it."

He leaned down and kissed me again. And I let him. There was no way he'd find me tomorrow so I might as well enjoy the hell out of this kiss. I'd kissed a lot of men in my time, and by far, this was the best. After a few seconds, I smiled against his lips and patted his chest. "You can kiss, Alex, I'll give you that. Hope that holds you over for a while."

"I think I can wait until tomorrow."

I chuckled and smiled up at him. "You won't find me, bub. You can't."

"Challenge accepted, beautiful."

He leaned down to kiss me again, but this time, I stopped him. "I'm going back inside."

Alex let me go and I walked back to the group. Macey and Dani were in the middle of heated debate about our favorite zombie show, while Booker watched with amusement at the varying opinions.

"Back me up, Pay," Macey demanded. "Daryl?"

"Sexy as hell," I said.

"Ew! No way," Dani said. "He's so…I don't know… just, no."

"What season are you on?" I asked.

"Just finished the first."

I chuckled. "Wait it out, Dani. You'll see."

"I think we'll stop where we are," Booker said.

Dani wrapped her arms around her husband's waist.

"Don't worry, honey, I'll never find anyone sexier than you."

He slipped his hand to the back of her neck and kissed her temple, but didn't comment. From the size of her grin, I figured they'd shared something secret.

"Um, can I confirm something with you?" I asked.

"Of course." Dani frowned. "Everything okay?"

"You wouldn't give my information to anyone, would you? Like my number or address?"

"No," Booker said. "Didn't matter who asked. You don't want your info out, we won't give it out."

I nodded. "Thanks."

"You got a problem with someone I need to take care of?"

"No. Thank you," I rushed to say. "If you don't share my information with anyone, there'll be nothing to take care of."

Booker looked at something over my head and I turned to see Alex watching us. I turned back toward Booker and forced myself not to smile in triumph.

"What have you done, missy?" Macey whispered.

"I haven't done anything," I whispered back. "That's the point."

She chuckled. "Can't wait to hear the story."

"I'll share everything on the way home."

"Deal." Macey raised an eyebrow. "Where's your wine?"

"Hmm. Must have lost it somewhere." I grinned.

"Well, let's get you some more."

"Lead the way," I said, and Macey grinned and headed to the kitchen.

* * *

"Ohmigod, Pay. He said all of that?" Macey asked as I drove home. We'd slipped out when Alex had put Lily to bed. The last thing I wanted him to see was which car I drove. He could trace me through my license plate if he had that ability.

"Yep." I nodded. "Weird, right?"

"Um, no, not weird necessarily."

"What?" I glanced at her when we stopped at a red light. "You're not thinking this is romantic are you?"

She shrugged. "Oh, I don't know. As long as he doesn't cross the line between romance and creepy stalker dude, then yeah, it's kind of romantic."

"Who are you and what have you done with my best friend?"

Macey laughed. "Dallas has reformed me."

"Remind me to hug him…or hit him next time I see him."

"You got it," she said. "So what are you going to do?"

"Nothing." I drove through the green light and headed to Macey's. "I don't have to do anything, right? He can't find me, so I'll just see him if I go to another party, which I won't for a while, by the way. So, it's all good."

Macey chuckled. "Okay, honey."

"What?"

"Nothing," she said, overly sweet and innocent like. "I'm just going to sit back and watch the show."

"I hate you so much right now."

"I know. And let me tell you, I'm loving *that*."

"Suck it, Mace."

"I plan to…when Dallas gets home."

"*Ew*! Mace! Ew, ew, ew."

She laughed and I pulled into the parking garage and into her extra space. I watched her as she continued to laugh, but she followed when I got out of the car, so I waited out her mirth which finally stopped once we'd walked into her apartment and poured wine.

The rest of the night was gratefully not on the subject of Alex 'Hawk' James.

THREE

Hawk

"**F**UCK!" I BELLOWED. It had been three weeks since I'd met Payton and I still hadn't been able to find her. I slammed my hand against the steering wheel, grateful Lily wasn't in the truck with me.

Payton had been right. I couldn't find her. Well, I could if Booker would give me any information, but he refused to, so I was fucked. She was officially a ghost. I didn't even have a last name. Booker wouldn't provide that either.

"Fuck!" I snapped again.

Unfortunately, I didn't have time to deal with the elusive Payton. I had three hours before I needed to relieve my sister from watching Lily, and I had a shit ton of work to do. I was currently in a Fred Meyer parking lot in Vancouver waiting to meet with my contact.

"Hawk, come in, over," Tammy's voice came over the

radio.

"I'm here, over."

"Kenny's sitting outside Starbucks. He's in a red hoodie, over."

"Copy, over."

I guided my truck to the spaces across from the coffee store and parked far enough away that I'd be somewhat obscured. As I climbed out of the cab and locked the doors, my eyes caught a glimpse of someone very familiar. My heart stuttered momentarily as I closed my eyes and opened them again to make sure I was seeing what I thought I was seeing. Payton was walking out the south door, one hand holding a grande coffee, the other her cell phone and purse. Her long, straight hair was pulled into a ponytail and she wore jeans, knee-high boots and a tight, cream turtleneck sweater that did incredible things for her tits.

I stepped closer to my truck and watched her as she climbed into her car and pulled out of her space. I grinned as I took down the license plate, along with the make and model of the car.

My little ghost had just materialized.

* * *

Payton

I pulled into my parents' driveway and turned off my car. After hitting Starbucks, I'd met Macey at Jantzen Beach and shopped for my nephew's birthday present. Billy was turning seven in a week and I had finally found him the video game he'd been begging for. I couldn't help but grin...I was going to be firmly in the favorite aunt category.

Popping the trunk, I stepped out of the car, my eyes on my purse as I dropped my keys into it and slung it over my shoulder.

"Hey, babe."

I squeaked, my phone dropping to the ground as I looked

up to see Alex walking toward me. He wore jeans, motorcy-cle boots, his vest and signature thermal. Lordy, lordy, he was gorgeous. "Wha—what are you doing here?"

He picked up my phone and handed it to me. "I told you I'd find you."

"And, uh, how…how did you do that exactly?" Again with the squeaking. Holy crap, I needed to get it together.

"Babe." Alex chuckled. "I did it and that's all you need to know."

"Okay," I said, and crossed my arms. "So, you've found me. Congratulations, you deserve a major award. But now that you've 'won,' what's the plan, handsome? Because I'm not really interested in a one night stand, and you're hell-bent on getting me out of your system, so you can see how this might be a conflict of interest, right?"

He smiled and I forced myself not to let out a sigh. "You and I are gonna get to know each other."

"We are?"

Alex nodded.

"And if *I* don't want to? Then what?"

He leaned against my car and raised an eyebrow. "You want to."

I took a deep breath, stuffing both the feeling of arousal and irritation. "Alex—"

"I fuckin' love it when you call me that."

"*Hawk*," I corrected.

"Don't do that, baby." Alex cupped my cheek. "Alt-hough, it's almost as sexy."

I stepped away from his touch. "Where's Lily?"

"She's with my sister."

"You have a sister?"

He nodded. "And a mother."

"You're close?"

"With my sister, yeah." He crossed his arms. "She's stayin' with me while she sorts shit out with her ex."

"Where's Lily's mother?"

Something scary crossed his face. Rage was far too simple to describe his expression.

"Sorry," I rushed to say. "It's none of my business."

"It's part of getting to know me," he said, although, he sounded irritated. "I don't know where her mother is. Honestly, I hope she's dead."

"Harsh."

"The whore is the biggest bitch on the planet, so, no, babe, it's not harsh enough."

I bit my lip. "Okay, right there is why I'm not sure this is a good idea."

Alex ran his thumb across my lip, tugging it from my teeth. "Break it down for me."

"You hate the woman who gave birth to your beautiful little girl. You don't seem interested in giving her the credit of at least gifting you with something incredible. Instead, you wish her dead. This doesn't bode well for someone like me who couldn't be less suited for you than any other woman on the planet. If you can't find even the tiniest bit of compassion for her, what happens to me when I do something you don't like? Will you wish me dead?"

"I'm not having this conversation with you in your parents' driveway."

"I don't think there's any point in having this conversation, period. I think you and I are ill suited to be anything other than acquaintances, so I wish you well, Alex James, but I think it's a good idea that we part ways."

He frowned. "Fuck, Payton. You're givin' up before we've even started!"

"Better now than to end up hurting each other later."

"I didn't peg you for a coward."

I knew he said this to goad me, but I wasn't particularly liking the emotions running through me, so I wasn't going to bite. I needed to stay strong, not allow the sadness of never seeing him again rule my actions. "Yep, I'm a coward. And if you knew anything about me, you'd pick up on that pretty quickly."

"What I'm pickin' up on, baby, is you're a shit liar." He smiled. "So, how about you come with me and we'll talk some more."

I let out an irritated groan. "Have you not heard a word I've said?"

"Have you eaten?"

"Alex."

He pushed away from the car, closing the distance between us. "Babe, have you eaten?"

My traitorous stomach rumbled. "No. But I'm just a step away from a food source, so I'm all good."

"Come eat with me." Alex took my hand and gave it a squeeze. "We'll talk."

"I don't do this, Alex."

"Pickin' up on that, Payton."

"Why are you pushing?" I demanded, but of course I still stood there holding his hand.

"Can't tell you why, babe, just know I have to."

I studied him. Wrong choice. He was far too gorgeous for his own good and staring at him just made me want to get naked, so I looked at my feet. But that brought into view his muscular legs and sexy as hell motorcycle boots, so I moved my eyes away, catching a glimpse of our hands entwined, a silver dog skull ring on his finger, and that just about had me kneeling before him. Gah! I was far too easy.

"Fine. Dinner," I said, and pulled out my cell phone. I texted my mom to let her know I wouldn't be home for a few hours, even though my car was in the driveway. My parents were out anyway, so it's not like they would be peeking out of the front room window to see who I was with, so I didn't give them any further information.

After locking up my car, I let Alex lead me to his truck. It wasn't old, but it was certainly beat up. He held the passenger door open for me and I had to climb into it, it was so high. As he made his way around the front of the truck, I took in the CB radio, grate between the front and back seats, and general disarray of the cab.

He climbed in beside me and started the engine.

"What do you do?" I glanced around the cab. "Assuming you do something outside of the club."

"Bounty hunter."

"Of course you are," I muttered under my breath.

Alex laughed. "I get better looking by the second, admit it."

"Wow," I said. "Cocky much?"

He didn't answer as he grinned and pulled away from the curb.

As we drove toward I-5, my phone rang and I pulled it out to find Macey calling. "Hey, Mace."

"Hey. Did I leave one of my bags in your trunk?"

"I have no idea," I said. "I'm actually not home right now, but I can check when I'm back."

"Where are you?"

"With Alex."

"Shut the front door. How did that happen?"

"No clue. He just showed up at home as I pulled in."

"Are you okay with that?" she asked. "'Cause I'll get Dallas to track you and pick you up if you want."

I glanced at Alex who raised an eyebrow at me before focusing back on the road.

"I'm fine, Mace. But I'll keep that in mind if he gets out of hand."

"I want details."

"It's just dinner."

"Still want details when you can talk," she said.

"Yeah, yeah." I smiled. "I'll call you later."

"'Bye," she said, and hung up.

I dropped my phone back in my purse and glanced at Alex again. "Why are you called Hawk?"

"I was a sharp shooter in the marines."

"Did you do any tours?"

"Two. Iraq."

"Wow," I whispered. "Thank you."

He took my hand, linking his fingers with mine. "You're welcome."

"Where are we going?"

"What do you feel like?"

"Typically on a first date, I'd say somewhere I can get a salad."

"But?" he countered.

"But, that's because I usually eat beforehand in an effort to keep the fact that I eat like a four-hundred pound man a secret for a while. And since I didn't do that, I'm in the mood for burgers, fries, and a big ass chocolate shake," I admitted. "You wanted to get to know me. Welcome to the show."

Alex laughed. "Burgerville it is."

He drove to the Salmon Creek location and pulled into the drive-thru.

"We're not going in?" I asked.

"Got a better place to eat."

"Let me guess. Some hidden and perfect place to hide a body?"

Alex laughed again. "Or fuck."

"Oh my god," I said, and pulled my hand away. "Don't be disgusting."

"Nothing about that is disgusting, Payton. Trust me. You're gonna love it."

"I'm not having sex with you, Alex," I snapped. "Did you actually think I would?"

"Don't get your panties in a wad, babe. I'm not expecting anything tonight except food and conversation." He smiled. "Besides, when I get you into bed, it'll be somewhere warm and very, very private. Somewhere I can take my time."

I shivered at the thought, swallowing several times before I found my voice. "You're not getting me into bed,

Alex."

"We'll see."

We pulled up and I ordered a Colossal, fries, and Chocolate Monkey. Alex ordered the pepper bacon burger and fries, along with a pop, and then we drove out of the parking lot. Alex headed down I-5 and exited at Jantzen Beach, but headed to the Marina rather than the mall.

He pulled into the parking lot and turned off the engine. "You got a coat?"

I shook my head.

"No problem," he said, and jumped out of the truck, opening the back door, and grabbing a leather jacket.

"We're eating here?"

"Yeah, babe."

I opened my door and gathered up the food, but before I could climb down from the cab, Alex was in front of me, taking my burdens from me and helping me out. He settled a ridiculously large leather jacket over my shoulders and then took my hand and the food and pulled me toward the pier.

"How do you have access to all of this?" I asked.

"I own a boat."

"You do not."

He smiled. "I do."

"What's the name of your boat?"

"Gravy."

I choked as I swallowed a laugh. "It is not."

He chuckled. "It is."

"That's probably the best thing I've ever heard."

Alex grinned again.

"My dad always says the only thing better than owning a boat is having a friend who owns one," I said.

Alex laughed. "There's a third option."

"There is?"

"Owning a boat and having recruits who have to pay their dues to look after the boat."

I chuckled. "You're smarter than you look, Alex James."

"Well, thank you, Payton Williams."

"Wow," I whispered as he pulled me to a stop in front of the prettiest (and largest) boat I'd ever seen. Granted, I wasn't well versed in boats, and had never personally been on one, other than one that pulled me when water skiing, but seriously, this was pretty. "Is this a yacht?"

"Yeah, babe. Technically it's a yacht." He smiled. "But I got it for a dinghy price."

"Permission to come aboard?" I retorted, and then blushed. "I heard that you're supposed to say that somewhere."

Alex laughed as he stepped onto the boat and reached his hand out to me. "You are fuckin' adorable."

I took his hand and he pulled me up. I landed against him and he steadied me. Before I could recover, however, he leaned down and kissed me. This kiss was so frickin' sweet, I had to fight not to give a fangirl sigh. Instead, I fell further against him and deepened the kiss.

It was Alex who broke the connection and settled his forehead against mine. "Fuckin' beautiful, Payton."

I closed my eyes. "I really need you not to be super nice to me right now, Alex. I'm trying to stick to my guns here and you're making it really difficult."

"I apologize," he said, but his voice was filled with humor. "Follow me."

We walked the perimeter of the boat and onto a deck that took in the lights of the restaurants across the Columbia. "This is beautiful," I said.

Alex set the food on a table on the deck. "Thanks. It's almost done."

"What do you mean? What more could you possibly do to it?"

"Not much," he admitted. "A few things in one of the cabins."

"Well it looks like a very posh yacht, Alex. Not sure what it used to look like, but it's beautiful."

"If you'd seen it when I bought it, you probably would have wondered if it was water worthy. A douchebag who had no respect for anything nearly destroyed this boat. It was a repo and the guy was pissed. I think his weapon of choice was a baseball bat. But I knew she could be fixed."

"How do you even go about finding a beat up yacht and get it for a dinghy price?" I asked, and sat at one of the benches against the railing. A small round table was bolted to the floor in front of me and it was where Alex had set the food.

"A buddy does repos."

"Ah." I unpacked the bags and sipped on my shake as Alex unlocked a door to what I assumed was where the sleeping quarters were, and turned on lights and grabbed blankets.

"You cold, babe?" he asked.

I shivered. "A little."

He gently wrapped a blanket around me, squeezing the back of my neck sweetly when he was done.

"Thanks." I smiled. "I didn't plan the shake part very well. Although, I don't regret it, even if the end result is frostbite."

Alex laughed and sat next to me. "I know a surefire way to get warm, babe."

"I bet you do."

He grinned and bit into his burger while I watched the lights shine off the water and picked at my fries.

"You okay?" he asked.

"Hmm-mm," I said, and smiled. "Just taking in the view. It's gorgeous."

"Yeah it is," he said, staring at me.

My cheeks heated. "Eat your food and stop being sweet."

"Glad you like it," he said.

"Technically, this is a warm place where you can take your time," I pointed out, internally slapping myself for bringing it up.

"Yeah, it is. I'll take you out soon, babe and we can stay overnight."

"I didn't say it to get you to take me out, Alex." I narrowed my eyes, although, there wasn't any heat behind it. "You're not getting me into bed, even with the promise of a day out on a gorgeous boat."

He laughed. "We'll see."

I pulled the blanket tighter around me. "What makes you so sure of yourself?"

"Don't know, babe." He studied me. "There's just something about you I can't shake."

I tipped my shake toward him. "Romantic."

Alex chuckled. "I'll work on that."

Pulling my legs up to my chest, I wrapped my arms around them, and settled my chin on my knees. "There's kind of something about you too, Alex."

"We'll get to know each other, yeah? Then go from there."

I shrugged. "I guess I don't have anything else better to do."

"Nice," he said, and sipped his pop. Setting the cup on the table, he reached out his hand. "Give me your phone."

"Why?"

"Want you to have my number in case you need me."

"I won't need you."

"Give me your phone, Payton."

I sighed and grabbed my purse, rummaging for the phone, and handing it to him. He tapped on the screen and then handed it back to me. I scrolled through and smiled. He'd saved his contact information under 'SMA.'

"SMA?"

He grinned. "Sexiest Man Alive."

I shook my head. "You're hilarious."

"True." He grinned. "And I'm right."

"We'll see."

"Yeah. We will."

"Where's Lily's mom?" I asked.

He sighed. "I don't know."

"Why did you break up?"

"We didn't."

I gasped. "You're still together?"

Alex let out a snort of derision. "Babe, we had nothin' to break up."

"Look, if you don't want to tell me, you don't have to. But we can't move forward unless I know something about you and your situation. I hate drama, Alex, and the last thing I want is the mess of a baby mama making things impossible."

He rubbed his forehead and then nodded. "Jenny was a club whore who I'd fucked a couple times. She wanted to be my old lady, I said no, so she got pregnant."

"On purpose?"

"Yeah. She thought I'd 'do the right thing,' but she's crazy, babe, and I wasn't interested in the drama either. When Lily was born, I checked paternity and confirmed she was mine. Shocked the hell out of me, 'cause she was sleeping with two or three other guys at the time."

"Wow. So, what did you do?"

"I got a fuckin' lawyer. We worked out child support, but when Jenny figured out I wasn't supporting her *and* Lily, and I sure as hell wasn't makin' her my old lady, she split. Lily was almost nine months old." He shook his head. "Bitch has been gone four years almost to the day. I don't know where she is, don't care. Just hope she's gone for good. Lily's better off."

"How did you feel about having to take care of Lily?"

"Babe, she's a little girl. She's *my* little girl. I was happy to take care of her. I just thank fuck she looks like me, not sure how I'd feel if I was lookin' at her mother every day."

I grimaced. "I guess that's honest."

"Life's too short to lie or candy coat shit. I'll protect my own. Whatever it takes, but I'll be honest doin' it."

"So what do we do about me? In regards to Lily."

He shifted in his seat. "We get to know each other. If this is goin' somewhere, we'll all spend time together. Before that, you and I'll be alone or we'll be low-key at the club if she's there."

"You've thought about this."

Alex chuckled. "Yeah, babe. I have."

"Do you know who I am? Who my brother is?"

"Yeah, Payton, I know. I did a full background check on you, so I know you more than you probably want me to."

I shrugged. "I don't have anything to hide, Alex. I'll probably do the same thing."

"Have at it, baby."

"So you know who my brother is and that doesn't concern you?"

"Club's clean, Payton. As am I…well, sort of. No felonies. Can't do my job without bending the law on occasion. Your brother stays out of my business, I'll stay out of his."

I rolled my eyes. "Brock doesn't typically get into anyone's business; well, outside of his job of course, unless he's also protecting one of his own. Then all bets are off."

"Noted." He cocked his head. "You really gonna make me wait?"

I choked on the shake I'd just sucked into my mouth. I slapped my chest and took a few deep breaths to calm the coughing. "You did *not* just ask me that."

"We're bein' honest, babe. Need to know where I stand."

"Um, yeah, I'm going to make you wait. I've never slept with anyone I wasn't in love with and you won't be the first."

He grasped his heart. "You wound me."

I chuckled. "You wanted honest, bub. You got honest."

He grinned and leaned forward. "I'll wait, baby, but that don't mean I'm not gonna wear you down." He slipped his hand to my neck and stroked my jaw. "And kissing better not be off the table, or we're gonna have a problem."

I licked my lips. "No, kissing's most definitely *not* off the table."

Hawk guided my legs to the ground and pulled me against him, lowering his mouth to mine. As he deepened the kiss, he slid his hand to my neck, and ran his thumb over my pulse. I loved kissing, had kissed a lot of boys and men in my day, but Alex was by far the best I'd ever experienced.

To me kissing was like holding hands…no big deal. Sex was different. It was intimate and when I slept with a man, it was because I thought there was the chance we'd last forever. There'd only been two that fell into that category for me and they'd both lasted several years, ending amicably.

But kissing Alex was different. I felt like he was giving me everything and I wanted to give him everything back. I broke the kiss and stroked his cheek as I tried to catch my breath. "You're freaking me out a little."

He smiled, his blue eyes soft and sweet. "Baby, there's no pressure. We're gettin' to know each other."

"I get that in theory, but you…" I shook my head, not wan-ting to finish my thought.

"What?"

Gah! I bit my lip. "You kiss me like that and I forget my manners."

Alex chuckled. "Well, I'm doin' it right then."

I rolled my eyes. "You're impossible."

"Won't ever make you do somethin' you don't want to, baby, but I fuckin' love kissin' you." He smiled. "And you just admitted you love kissin' me, so, gonna make that work for me."

"It works, handsome. Just might work a little too well."

He grinned and kissed me again, until his phone interrupted the moment. "Hey, Kayla. Lily okay?" he asked, and wrapped an arm around me, pulling me against him. "Yeah. Probably in a couple of hours. Put her on." I snuggled closer to Alex as he talked on the phone. "Hey, baby. No, I'll be home after you go to bed. You being good for Kayla?" He chuckled. "Kisses back. Love you to the moon, baby girl. Okay. Put auntie back on." He kissed my temple and gave me a gentle squeeze. "You okay? Sure? Yeah, really appreciate it, Kay. Yeah." He chuckled. "Okay. 'Bye."

"You're really sweet, Alex."

"Don't tell anyone that, baby. Bounty hunters aren't supposed to be sweet."

I chuckled. "My lips are sealed."

"What's your work schedule over the next few weeks?"

"I'm working all week." I craned my head to look up at him. "Then the following week, school's out Wednesday through Friday for Thanksgiving week, but otherwise, I'm typically working until about four every day."

"Right, Thanksgiving."

I smiled. "Do you have plans?"

"Usually go to the club."

"Are you committed to that?" I asked.

"Not necessarily. Why?"

"Because you're welcome to join us. We cook a buttload of food and there's football and pie. A lot of pie." I smiled. "Plus a gaggle of kids to keep Lily occupied. Your sister's welcome too."

"Let's play it by ear, yeah?"

I nodded and stared out at the water. I couldn't explain it, but the fact that he didn't jump at the chance to spend Thanksgiving with me really disappointed me. I'd been hesitant to get involved with him and yet, here I was sad that he wanted to play it by ear.

Obviously, I was insane.

Or a woman.

Sometimes I wondered if there was much difference.

"You okay?" he said against my ear.

"Hmm-mm."

"You gonna share what's pissed you off?"

I frowned up at him. "I'm not pissed off."

He studied me for a few seconds. "Somethin's off,

babe."

I sighed, pulling away from the warmth of his body and facing him. Settling my chin on my drawn up knees again, I forced a smile. "I'm working out my feelings, Alex. You've just gotta give me a little time."

"I'm givin' you an out for Thanksgiving, babe."

"What do you mean?"

"We're playin' it by ear so you can un-invite me if you want to."

I sat up. "Why would I un-invite you?"

He chuckled. "Because you're workin' out your feelings. You might decide you're not ready for your very stable family to meet my equally unstable one."

I wrinkled my nose. "Well, thanks for putting words in my mouth."

"I'm not lookin' to put words in your mouth or start a fight, babe. Just want to give you an out."

"Well, I don't want an out," I said. "You are officially invited to Thanksgiving."

"Okay." He grinned. "I'll check with my sister, but that sounds good. Thank you."

Our awkward moment was broken when my phone pealed in the silence. I dug in my purse and pulled it out. "Hello."

"Hey, honey, just checking to see when you'll be home," my mom said.

"Probably in a couple of hours. Everything okay?"

"Of course. Just like to know when my chickens are back in the coop."

I chuckled. "I'm the only chicken, Mom. Everyone else was smart enough to fly away."

"I'm waiting for everyone to come back."

"Good luck with that."

"Dad and I are going to watch a movie, so just text me when you're inside and have locked up."

"Will do. Hey, I've invited a couple of friends for

Thanksgiving, is that a problem?"

"The more the merrier, honey. We'll discuss details the week of."

"Sounds good. I'll see you in the morning."

"Okey doke. Love you."

I smiled. "Love you too, Mom. 'Bye." I hung up and dropped my phone back into my purse.

"What was it like livin' in a Cleaver house?"

I shrugged. "I wish I could say something profound and deep that would sum everything up, but honestly, it was awesome. We're all still really close. I'm guessing your home life wasn't so good?"

"Dad's in jail for sex crimes against the foster kids my parents took in and my mom didn't do a fuckin' thing to stop it, so yeah, mine wasn't so good. But it's done, so I don't dwell."

"I'm sorry, Alex. That sucks." I squeezed his arm. "It sounds like you're making things really happy for Lily, though. You're breaking a cycle of sorts."

"Yeah." He stood. "You done?"

"Um, yeah."

"Okay, I'll take you home."

"O-okay," I stuttered. Apparently he was working out his feelings too, and the subject of his life was not a good one, so I didn't press.

I folded the blanket he'd wrapped around me and handed it back to him before gathering my stuff up while he locked up the boat. Alex helped me back onto the pier and then released my hand and I was forced to jog to catch up to him. "Alex, wait."

He stopped, but didn't turn around.

"What just happened?" I asked.

He faced me, his face impassive. "What do you mean?"

"I don't play that game, Hawk. You know exactly what I mean. If you don't want to talk about it right now or want to revisit it later, I'm fine with that, but don't act dumb, and if you say 'nothing,' in answer to any of my questions that start with 'what's wrong?' I will maim you."

"I don't want to talk about it right now."

"Is it something I said?"

"Fuck, Payton, you just said you'd be fine with that answer."

"I am…" *sort of,* "…so long as I didn't do something to offend you."

He shook his head. "You didn't do anything to offend me. Can we go now?"

I nodded and followed him again, this time able to stay in sync with him, however, he still didn't touch me. He held the door of the truck open, waited for me to climb up, and then made his way to the driver's side.

The drive home was excruciating. He said nothing. Nada, zip, nuttin' honey. Just focused on the road. I originally thought I might have hit a nerve on the boat, but now I was spiraling into all manner of offenses…only stopping with the possibly I'd killed his pet in a past life.

See? Crazy.

Alex pulled up to my house and turned off the truck. I slipped out of his jacket and set it on the console between us. "Thanks for dinner."

"Hey." He grabbed my hand. "Workin' shit out, yeah?"

I nodded.

"Call you next week."

I nodded again.

He tugged me forward, but I pulled away from him. "I'm not kissing you in front of my parents' house, Alex. Not yet, anyway."

"So, it's fuckin' payback time, huh?"

"What?" I snapped. "*No.*"

"Let me guess. Your dad would go ape-shit over you datin' someone like me, right?"

"No, not at—"

"Fine, babe. We'll do it your way."

"*God*, you make me crazy." I let out a frustrated growl. He moved to leave the truck but I pulled him back. "Wait. This conversation isn't done."

"No?"

"No," I snapped. "I don't want to kiss you in front of anyone until we know where we're going with this. It has nothing to do with my dad. And for your information, my dad isn't like that. He knows me enough to know that if I want to date someone, it's my decision and he trusts me to make it. Brock, on the other hand…"

"Fuck," he whispered.

"I'm gonna go."

"Wait, babe." Alex grabbed my hand. "I'm sorry."

"Thank you."

"You really not gonna kiss me?"

I couldn't stop a sigh of relief as I shook my head. "Does it make you feel better to know I want to just as much as you do?"

"Doubtful," he grumbled.

I squeezed his hand. "I'm sorry if I said something earlier."

"You didn't."

"Yeah, the silent treatment the whole way home proved that."

Alex sighed. "Babe, you sayin' shit like I'm 'breakin' the cycle' drives home the fact that I'm fuckin' failin' at it."

"So I *did* say something."

"Fuck me, Payton. You ever not intuitive?"

"I'm paid to be intuitive," I said. "It makes me a good teacher."

He nodded. "Look. You have a charmed life, good family, fuckin' great friends—"

"And you don't?"

"It's different, Payton. My club's my family outside of Kayla and Lily. Before the club, I never had friends I could trust like you can trust yours." He dragged his hands through his hair. "I know I'm fuckin' Lily up big time. Shit, her teacher even said she's behind in her language skills and asked me if I read to her at night…like if I don't, I should be ashamed."

"And do you?"

"If I'm home…sometimes. But not always." He frowned. "I'm not breakin' any cycles, babe. I'm just makin' new ones to fuck up my daughter."

"So I hit a nerve," I observed, and smiled.

"Yeah, babe, you hit a nerve."

"Can I put my two cents in regarding Lily…purely from a professional standpoint?"

"Have at it."

"Okay, I'm not sure why her teacher would say she's behind in her language skills. Yes, she sometimes says words a little softer than other girls her age, has some difficulty saying her r's, but she forms full and coherent sentences and understands what you're saying to her, so in my opinion, she's right on track. She also has a pretty good sense of what people she can trust, considering I heard her crying for a little while in the store before she stopped and talked to me. She inherently knew I'd help her. I think her teacher is either an insensitive cow, or wants to offer up her personal services to help Lily in the hopes of getting in your pants."

It took him a second to respond but then he let out a booming laugh that filled the cab of the truck. I was so distracted by the sound, I didn't register him reaching for me until his mouth was on mine and I was melting into his arms.

I broke the kiss and dropped my forehead to his arm. "Alex."

"In less than five minutes, you've erased the fear I've had for years, babe." He stroked my cheek. "I won't apologize for kissin' you."

I met his eyes. "I was just telling you the truth. I do think Lily's perfectly fine. If she wasn't, I'd say that too."

He kissed me again.

"Alex," I said, smiling against his lips. "You can't keep kissing me when I tell you the truth. Our mouths will be permanently attached if that's the case."

"Explain why that would be a problem," he retorted.

"Just imagine trying to track down some bad guy with my mouth attached to yours."

He grinned. "Minor point made…maybe."

I rolled my eyes. "Do you need more examples?"

"I'm good." He smiled at me. A smile that went to my soul.

"I need to go," I whispered, shifting away from him.

He nodded and reached for my hand again. "Thanks, babe."

I smiled. "Not sure what I did, but you're welcome."

He climbed from the cab, made his way to my side, and pulled open the door. I jumped down and grabbed my purse, hitting the trunk button on my key fob.

"Want some help?" Alex asked.

"No, I'm good. Just have to see if Macey left a bag," I said, and peered inside. "Which she did." I pulled our shopping bags out and then closed the trunk.

"Thanks for tonight, babe," Alex said, and smiled.

"I'm always up for burgers and boats."

He chuckled. "I'll keep that in mind."

"Will I see you before Thanksgiving?"

"Babe, Thanksgiving's over a week away."

"You say that like I'm not aware of that fact," I retorted.

"Yeah, you'll see me before Thanksgiving. I'll call you."

"Maybe I'll answer."

He raised an eyebrow. "You'll answer."

I smirked. "We'll see, handsome."

"I'm gonna kiss you, babe."

"Nope," I said even as I raised my head.

He chuckled and bent part of the way, forcing me to stand on tiptoe to reach him. "You're a butt," I said just before his mouth covered mine.

I found the bags in my hands obtrusive, especially since I wanted to touch him, so I dropped them to the ground and wove my fingers into his hair. I was grateful it was dark, but even if it hadn't been, I wouldn't have objected. There was something about kissing Alex James that made me want more. I liked him. A lot.

I forced myself to break the kiss, dropping my forehead to his chest. He pulled me closer, tugging gently on my ponytail. I raised my head so I could meet his eyes. "You're still a butt."

He chuckled. "Told you I was going to wear you down."

"Hmm-mm. We'll see." I picked up my bags again and rifled through my purse for my keys.

"Sure I can't help you carry those?"

I shook my head. "I'm good."

"I'll wait for you to get inside."

"Okay." I smiled. "Thanks for dinner."

"Anytime, babe," he said, and I let myself inside, leaning against the door for a minute to catch my breath.

I fired off a text to my mom to let her know I was home, and then one to Macey to let her know I had her stuff. Then I locked up, set the alarm, and headed to my room with a glass of wine. Time to process.

FOUR

Payton

ALMOST A WEEK later, I was walking out of school when my phone rang. I grimaced to see '*SMA*' pop up on the screen. I almost ignored it. He'd waited six days to call me and, if I was being honest, I was hurt that he hadn't called sooner. I thought we'd had a connection, but when day three, then four, then five passed without a phone call, I thought I was wrong.

Unfortunately, the truth was I'd missed him, so I answered. "Hello?"

"Hey, baby."

I shivered as his voice washed over me. "Alex?" I played dumb.

"You busy tonight?" he asked.

"Yes."

"Seriously?" He sounded surprised and a little annoyed.

"Seriously," I said. "I have plans with Macey. Why, what's up?"

"Can you blow her off?"

I snorted. "*No.*"

"I wanted to take you out on the boat."

"Well, then you can plan a day that works for me and we can go from there."

He sighed. "Don't get all pissy, Payton. It was just a question."

"Was it just a question, Hawk? Because I was thinking you decided I was going to drop everything at your beck and call." I unlocked my car and climbed inside. "It's girls' night out, which trumps you, handsome."

"You pissed at me?"

Ohmigod, talk about clueless. "Why would I be pissed at you?"

"Okay, babe. You have fun tonight. I'll call you tomorrow."

Then he was gone. He hung up. I let out a frustrated squeal as I started my car and pulled out of the parking lot. I made it home in record time. I was probably irritated enough to speed, but I'd deny it if anyone asked.

My parents wouldn't be home from work for a while, so I had plenty of uninterrupted time to shower and change for girls' night out, and even had the minute chance of getting out the door before they arrived. Dani and her best friend were joining us, along with my sister-in-law, Bailey, and then Bailey and I were crashing at Macey's place, so I packed a bag before jumping in the shower. Dinner and live music was the plan and it was at a place you didn't have to dance if you didn't want to. I was more of a homebody, so I would more than likely watch from the sidelines…well, unless I drank a little too much. Then all bets were off.

Once I'd applied my makeup and dried my hair, I set it in hot curls while I pulled out my second favorite little black dress. The stretchy material formed a fitted bodice and flared skirt that stopped just above my knees, while a sheer mesh décolletage sculpted a sweetheart silhouette. The open back had crisscrossing straps which tied in a pretty bow at the center which made me feel feminine and fun at the same time.

I did own a sexier dress, but I wasn't really looking for attention, wanted or otherwise, tonight. I just wanted to hang with my girls.

This thought brought Alex to mind and I shook my head. The pull of a night out on his boat was definitely tempting, but I didn't bail on my friends and I certainly didn't ask 'how high?' when a man said 'jump.' It just wasn't me. Even if the man *was* sexy as hell.

After completing my ensemble with my very favorite four-inch pair of cherry red Jimmy Choos (a *major* splurge on my part), I grabbed my purse, bag, and coat, and headed upstairs. The house was still pretty much dark, so I knew my parents weren't home. Setting the alarm, I let myself out and locked the door.

"Fuck me, babe, you take forever to get ready."

I squeaked and dropped my stuff, turning to find Alex sitting on my front porch. "Ohmi*god*, Hawk, you can't keep doing that to me."

He chuckled as he stood and picked up my discarded items. "You look beautiful, Payton."

"Thank you. What are you doing here?" I demanded, ignoring the little flutter of delight that was spreading through my body. He looked delicious, his jeans painted on, a black thermal and leather jacket that made me want to peel his clothes off of him.

"Taking you to girls' night."

"Come again?" I shivered, having underestimated just how cold it was outside.

"Why aren't you wearing your coat?"

"I never do when I'm driving. It's too constricting."

He took my coat still draped over my arm and helped me into it. "Well, now I'm driving, so you can stay warm."

"You can't take me to girls' night, Hawk."

"Yeah I can."

"Hawk, I don't hear from you for days and now you expect me to go with you because you show up here?" I studied him. "Who does that?"

He shook his head. "Babe, I was a dick."

"Ya think?" I retorted.

"Let me make it up to you."

I narrowed my eyes. "How exactly?"

"I'll drive you wherever you want to go. Pick you up. You can drink all night and I'll make sure you're safe. If you're wasted, I'll bring you home if you want, take you back to the club or get a hotel room."

"So you're trying to get me drunk and into bed?"

He cocked his head. "Now you're just being ornery."

I bit back a laugh. He was right. I was being ornery. "I'm staying at Macey's tonight, so I have to drive or I'll have no way to get home tomorrow."

"I'll pick you up tomorrow and we can spend the day together, or I can drive you home if you have other plans."

"Alex," I whispered.

"There she is," he said, and slid his hand to my neck.

"What?"

"You call me Hawk when you're irritated, handsome when you're beyond pissed, and Alex when you're back to liking me."

"I do?"

He chuckled. "You do, babe."

"I have a tell?" I let out a mock huff. "Damn it!"

Alex laughed and I couldn't help but smile. "I'm your driver for the night, baby, yeah?"

"What about Lily?"

"She's with Kayla."

"She's okay with that?"

"Baby, I've had a shit week, Lily's been sick and I took some time off, which meant I've been behind. Kay was happy to do this for me because I needed to see you."

"So that's why you didn't call?"

"Yeah," he said. "I probably picked up my phone a hundred times, but baby girl took all my attention. Will you let me make it up to you?"

"You really don't mind?"

He dropped his forehead to mine. "I really don't mind."

I smiled. "Okay. Thank you."

This is when he kissed me and it was *good*. So good, I didn't want it to end, so I wrapped my arms around his waist and up his back. Finally! God, I'd missed this. He took his time and I didn't want it to end. However, the lights of my dad's car pulling into the driveway had me pushing Alex away like an errant teen. "Damn it! Let's go."

"I take it this is your dad?"

"Yep." I grabbed my purse from his hand and slung it over my shoulder. "I'll meet you at your truck."

He shook his head. "Ah, no."

"What?" I frowned, trying to push him from the porch. "Go."

"Baby, I'm not running from your dad like we're kids doin' somethin' we're not supposed to be doing."

"Then what do you propose?"

"Oh, I don't know," Alex droned. "How about I meet him like a man?"

The garage door raised and I heard my dad drive inside. Maybe he'd just go into the house…maybe he didn't even notice us.

"No. Absolutely not. I had this all planned for Thanksgiving. You were going to meet him and everyone then." I yanked my coat closer to my body. "You're not meeting him on the darkened front porch just as I'm scurrying away."

"Baby, you're not scurrying anywhere." He frowned. "You fuckin' ashamed of me?"

"What? No." I shook my head. "No. Alex, I'm sorry. This isn't what this is about."

"Pay?" my dad called as he locked his car. "That you?"

Or maybe not.

"Yeah, Dad. I'm just heading out the door to meet Macey. Alex came to pick me up." My dad appeared before us and I smiled. "How was your day?"

He looked Alex up and down, but not in a judgy way, just in my Dad sizing up my man-friend kind of way. "It was good, honey. How about yours?"

"Good. Um, Dad, this is Alex. Alex, Dad."

My dad reached out his hand and Alex took it. "Nice to meet you."

"Nice to meet you too, son." Dad glanced back at the street. "Is that your truck?"

"Yeah."

"It's a good truck. Safe. Just how I want my daughter to be."

Alex grinned, his hand settling at the base of my spine. "Couldn't agree more."

"You staying at Macey's tonight?" my dad asked me.

"Yep. Brock and Dallas are gone, so Bailey's staying too."

Dad nodded. "Good deal. You need me, you call."

"I will, Dad," I said, and kissed his cheek. "Thanks."

He hugged me and then smiled at Alex. "I think we understand each other."

Alex nodded. "Yeah."

Dad let himself into the house as Alex grabbed my stuff and guided me to his truck. "Your dad's pretty laid back."

I settled myself in the truck and saw the front curtain flutter. "Yeah, sort of. He's got my cell phone tracked as we speak and he's watching from the front window."

Alex laughed. "Good to know."

He threw my stuff in the back and then climbed up beside me and started the truck.

"So, what happened with Lily?" I asked as he pulled away from the curb.

"Croup. I was worried it was whooping cough, but she

was immunized, so the doctor said she'd just be uncomfortable until the virus left her system. A couple nights sitting in a steamy bathroom seemed to do the trick."

"Still scary though."

He nodded. "She went back to school today and really wanted to spend time with her aunt, so I used the distraction."

"You had to take time off work?"

"Yeah, three days. Kayla took Monday for me, so I could at least get a little work done. But unless Lily was sleeping, she was attached to me. It's gonna take me a week to just get caught up. I love her, but man, I was ready for a break."

I chuckled. "I get it. My nieces are the same way with my brothers-in-law. Something about little girls and their daddies."

"And you? Were you a daddy's girl?"

"Oh, hell, yes. When I was sick, all I wanted was my dad." I smiled. "He used to give me M&Ms and tell me they were magical medicine."

"I haven't tried that."

"It worked every time, until I figured out that if I "played" sick, I'd get M&Ms. Mom shut that down pretty quick."

Alex laughed. "Fuckin' A, the emotional blackmail girls can dish out."

"Quit paying the ransom and maybe we'll stop."

"Never gonna happen." He linked his fingers with mine. "It's way too much fun."

I grinned, my heart light as we drove into Portland. "Did you ever visit Booker?"

"Not at his place, no."

"But you know where he lives."

"Yeah, babe."

"Are you guys friends outside of the club?" I asked.

He let out a weird sound. Chuckle? No, maybe snort. Chortle? Yes, it was definitely a chortle.

I squeezed his hand. "What?"

"Booker was one of the kids my parents' took in to foster. He and I have a complicated past."

"I didn't realize he was a foster child," I said sadly.

"He had a shit life, baby. It's why he works so hard to make his current one good."

"Why is your relationship complicated? Are you not friends?"

"We're gettin' there," Alex said. "My dad molested most of the girls who came through our house. I didn't know about it until Annie. She made a formal complaint through CPS, but it got lost or buried, or something. Not sure. Booker hacked into the computers and found it. It set in motion a series of events that sent my dad to prison for a very long time."

"And you blame Booker for that?"

"Fuck, no. I hated my dad, but as a kid, I didn't know just how much of a bastard he was. He used to smack my mom around and me too, 'til I got big enough to defend myself, but I still didn't know the depths of evil in him. Booker nailed him to the wall. I was thankful for it."

"So, why the tension?"

"The issue came when Annie got pregnant by some douchebag in high school and had an abortion that went bad. Booker thought I'd knocked her up, so he's hated me for years. We're cool now, but can't say we're gonna share our feelings anytime soon."

I smiled. "No, that'll probably take some time."

"Where am I parking?"

I looked out the windshield to see we were almost at our destination. "I have Macey's code, so we can park in her extra space."

He nodded and guided the truck into the underground parking structure and I directed him to the space. I pulled out my phone. "I just have to check with Macey and make sure she's comfortable with you coming up."

"I don't bite."

"No, I know. It's not that." I wasn't sure what to say at this point. It's not as though Macey's life was a secret, but I also didn't want to drag her shit out onto the street so to speak.

He sighed. "It's fine, babe. I'm a lot to take."

"She was raped."

"Fuck," he rasped.

I grimaced. "It's been almost three years since it happened and for the most part, it's done, but she gets nervous around men she doesn't know and it's why we rally around her when Dallas is gone. Usually Bailey or I stay with her so she doesn't have to be alone. The guy broke into her old apartment, so she doesn't always feel safe when she's by herself."

"Understandable."

I nodded.

"I don't have to come up, Payton. I can wait in the lobby, or here in the truck. Whatever she feels comfortable with. I can even hang at Booker's place until you're ready."

"Thank you. I'll see how she feels and go from there." I texted Macey to let her know what was happening and she responded immediately. "She said that Dani and Booker are already there, so she's fine with you coming up."

"It's a party, apparently."

I grinned. "I wouldn't be surprised if Bailey and Brock are also there already. I'm usually late, so Brock said he'd take Bailey." I checked my phone. "I'm only twenty-two minutes late tonight, and I probably would have been on time if a certain badass biker dude didn't delay me."

Alex laughed. "Next time I'll make the wait a little more enjoyable."

"Good lord, the thought of you ever making anything more enjoyable might kill me."

Having released his seatbelt, he leaned forward and kissed me. I was still locked in, but not for long. Still holding my lips hostage, he freed me from my belt and pulled me onto his lap. I slipped my fingers into his hair and slid my tongue into his mouth, deepening the kiss.

Alex held me close, but I couldn't get close enough and groaned in frustration as I cupped his face.

"Baby," he said between kisses, "I'm not fuckin' you in the truck in a parking garage. You need to quit with those noises."

I leaned back and frowned. "What noises?"

Alex cocked his head. "You don't know?"

"I groaned because I was frustrated…obviously not helping the situation," I said.

"No, babe, before that. Never mind."

"What?" I said and gripped his shoulders. "Tell me."

He chuckled. "I just thought you were gonna come."

I slapped his arm. "I do *not* sound like I'm going to come when I'm kissing someone, Hawk. That's disgusting."

He cupped my bottom and gave it a gentle squeeze. "You do when you're kissin' me."

"I do not." My face flamed. "Let me go."

"No."

"Hawk," I warned, and tried to shift off his lap.

"Payton, settle," he said. "Don't be embarrassed baby. Nothin' about what we're doin' should embarrass you."

"You just said I sound like I'm having an orgasm while I'm kissing someone. Now I'm thinking back to all of the other men I've kissed and wondered how many times I've done that without knowing."

Alex's body stiffened. "How many guys have you kissed?"

"Several."

"Fuck me, Payton."

"Well, you asked! I've kissed a lot of guys, Hawk. But I've only slept with two. And they were two men I loved very much once upon a time, and with whom I'm still friends. Neither of them mentioned noises when I kissed them…I barely made noises when we had sex, so I'm sorry if this is taking me a bit by surprise."

He looked at me like I was an alien. "You didn't make noise when you came? Ever?"

I pushed at his shoulders again. "I'm not having this conversation with you."

"Babe, tell me."

"No. I don't kiss and tell, Hawk. I like to keep my past my past."

"Payton?"

"What?"

"Did they make you come?"

I gasped. "What? That's none of your business."

He frowned. "They didn't make you come."

"I'm not taking the bait, Hawk. It's none of your business."

"Okay, baby, we'll leave it there for now."

"Forever," I said.

"For now." He patted my bottom. "How do I get Alex back?"

"Stop being such a jerk." My phone buzzed but I ignored it.

"Okay, baby." He smiled, and honestly I had no idea why he was so smug. "I'll stop being a jerk."

"What are you up to?" I asked, narrowing my eyes at him.

He laughed. "God, you're gorgeous, Payton."

My phone buzzed again. "Stop being sweet and tell me what you're up to."

"I'm not up to anything, babe. Promise." He picked up my phone that was sitting on the seat beside us. "We should get upstairs."

Just to drive home his point, my phone buzzed again. I snatched it from him and checked my texts, still sitting in his lap, mind you. I liked sitting here. Gah! I was insane.

"Let's go," I said, still looking at my phone, but he held

firm. "What?"

"Hey," he whispered. "Look at me."

I met his eyes and bit my lip.

"I like everything about you, baby, yeah? Don't ever feel self-conscious or embarrassed about your responses to me. We're new. We're figurin' shit out." He stroked my cheek. "You're beautiful, Payton."

I sighed. "And you're back to being sweet."

Alex chuckled. "Come here."

He drew my head down for another delicious kiss, but this time I made sure I didn't make any noise whatsoever.

"Don't like that, baby," he said, and broke the kiss.

I scowled. "Now I'm not kissing right?"

"Your kissin's fine, baby. It's you all locked up and stiff."

"You could tell?"

"Yeah, Payton I could tell." He smiled. "I want you to let go. Just let it happen, yeah?"

"I'll think about it. But right now, we have to get upstairs." I scooted off his lap and was relieved when he let me.

FIVE

Payton

I CLIMBED OUT of the truck before he could make it to my side and waited for him to grab my stuff from the back. Once he had my bag, he took my hand and we headed to the elevator and up to the lobby.

There was a new doorman, apparently, so we went through the normal process of signing in and getting permission to ride up to Macey's floor, but we did it without the friendly banter that I normally had with the other doormen. I was glad, however, this new person was as diligent as the others.

I knocked on my old apartment door and my brother pulled it open. "Nice of you to join us, sissy," he said, and pulled me in for a hug.

"Shouldn't you be gone by now?" I asked.

He chuckled. "Soon."

I felt Alex's hand on my lower back and pulled away from my brother. "Brock, this is Alex."

My brother eyed him up and then shook his hand. "We've met."

"You have?" I asked.

"Yeah, long story," Alex said.

"Where have you been for the last twenty minutes?" Macey demanded as she walked into the living room. "You texted to say you were here like six days ago."

I chuckled. "You're funny."

She hugged me and then smiled at Alex. "Hey, Hawk."

"Hey, babe."

I introduced Alex to everyone he didn't know, which was pretty much only Bailey. Alex got around it would seem. Dani, Kim, and Booker were already there, so Booker and Alex gravitated to one another while the rest of us reconnected. Dani looked gorgeous in her killer dark blue dress, knee-length and low-cut that showcased her very full chest…I'd die for boobs that big, alas, I was stuck with my B-cups…and a dark blue pair of peep toe boots that showed off her shapely calves.

Kim was new to me and she was gorgeous. I was sure she must be a model, because she was tall, probably five-foot-ten or eleven, with killer legs that went on for days. She had long dark hair, soft brown eyes, and full lips that seemed to be in a permanent smile. She wore a skin-tight tiny black dress that stopped just below her butt and stiletto boots that went up past her knees, emphasizing her long legs, and she was super sweet.

"Can I get you a beer?" Dallas asked Alex.

"Nah, I'm good."

"Okay, honey, you can go," Macey said.

"In a bit," Dallas said. "Where are you going?"

"I was thinking *Blush*," Dani said.

"Fuck me," Booker said.

"Too soon?" she asked, and Kim started laughing.

"I'll host you at *Blush*," Booker said. "But another time when I can keep an eye on you."

Dani smirked. "Killjoy."

There was obviously a story there and I couldn't wait to find out what it was.

"We're going to Mississippi Studios," Macey said. "Under Oaks and the City Suns are playing."

"Then where?" Brock asked.

"You're on assignment all night, honey. Or did you forget?" Bailey said, smiling up at him.

"So?" Brock countered.

Bailey rolled her eyes at me. "So, we'll be fine."

"Hey, big brother, we can take care of ourselves you know," I said. "Hawk's playing chauffeur tonight."

"And I got Dani and Kim," Booker said.

As the group talked logistics and my fellow girl posse objected to the sudden need for babysitters, I turned toward Alex and narrowed my eyes at him. He smiled, but he looked guilty.

Grabbing his arm, I faced the group and forced a smile. "Excuse us for a minute." Before anyone could respond, I dragged him into the hallway and crossed my arms. "When did all of this come about?"

"What?"

"You know what." I paced the hall, waving my finger at him. "I'm just curious…do you have to touch your magic rings together to physically become the Super Protecto Twins?"

"Babe." Alex laughed. "What the hell are you talking about?"

"If you put on glasses, would I suddenly fail to recognize you?"

"Payton."

He sounded a little peevish, but I was going for contrite.

"There is *one* thing I've always wondered, handsome." I paused in my pacing and settled my hands on my hips. "Do y'all *have* to wear those tights? Are they government regulation, an aerodynamic thing…or just a lifestyle choice?"

"Fuck me," he whispered as he dragged his hands through his hair.

"So, you didn't offer to drive just because you were being sweet and wanted to make anything up to me, you are essentially a glorified bouncer." Okay, now he was looking mildly contrite. "Right. No argument. Got it."

"If I could speak, Payton, then I could explain."

"Don't bother. Go home, Hawk." All manner of emotion flooded me. Irritation that he had ulterior motives to seeing me tonight, anger that he felt I needed to be watched and he'd obviously planned something with Booker…or worse yet, my brother…and then, just plain hurt. This last emotion deflated me somewhat. Partly because I didn't want to feel hurt by someone I hardly knew. It brought to light that I'd once again misread the situation, something I didn't do, and thought he felt the same way I did. At this point, I was resigned. If I continued on the path I was on, I'd get dizzy with wondering whether 'he loves me, he loves me not.' I had to cut him loose and move on or I'd be in a constant state of emotional nausea.

"Babe."

"Just go," I whispered, and pushed past him to go back in-side.

Macey was at my side immediately, wrapping an arm around me, and guiding me to her bedroom. "Are you okay?"

"Yep."

"Then why are you crying?"

I gasped. "I'm not."

She grinned and pointed to my face. "Okay, not totally, but you have a little wetness there."

"Bite me, Macey!"

She laughed, which meant I did too. Gotta give it to my best friend, she knew how to get me out of my head.

"So, what happened?" she asked.

I sighed and flopped into the chair by the window. "He

lied. No biggie.”

Macey smiled and sat in the matching chair next to mine. “How did he lie?”

“He told me he’d call me. He didn’t. Granted, Lily was sick, so I get why he couldn’t. And I thought he was being super sweet when he showed up on my porch, all romantic and crap, saying he missed me and that he wanted to make this week up to me. But now I find out this watchdog crap was all planned. *Planned*, Mace. His sweetness was all under the guise of backing up his “brother” to keep Dani and Kim safe.” I shook my head. “And my feelings are hurt. Damn it, Macey, I don’t get my feelings hurt this soon. Boys suck!”

“It had nothin’ to do with Dani and Kim, Payton,” Alex said. He was leaning against the doorframe, his arms crossed, his face unreadable.

I squeaked. “Stop doing that!”

“I’ll give you a minute, hmm?” Macey said, and rose to her feet.

“No, it’s all good,” I countered, sinking further into the chair. “Hawk was just leaving.”

He smirked. “I’m not goin’ anywhere, Payton.”

Macey smiled down at me and I glared up at her. “If you leave this room, Macey Stone, I will kill you. Like as in dead, dead. Not figuratively, *literally*. Murder, Macey. *Murder*. I will commit it.”

“Okay, honey. I only ask you make it quick.” Macey grinned and started toward the door.

“I won’t. I’ll make you suffer.”

She slid past Alex and he closed the distance between us, sitting in the seat Macey had just vacated and settling his ankle on his knee.

“Don’t get comfortable, bub, you’re not staying.”

“Payton, you’re overreacting.”

“Don’t tell me I’m overreacting, Hawk. I get to feel how I feel.” I scowled at him. “Do you know *nothing* about women? God, you're infuriating!"

He smiled at me. Smiled! Gah!

"Break it down for me, baby."

"No."

"Babe, you gotta work with me here, or this isn't gonna work."

I shrugged. "It's *not* going to work. I'm calling it."

Alex chuckled. "You're callin' nothin', baby."

"I am." I stood and faced him. "We're just too different, Alex. It's okay. I've enjoyed getting to know you. I hope we can be friends."

I watched his face as he stared up at me. His expression gave nothing away, but his eyes. God, his eyes. I bit my lip, hoping the pain would bring me to my senses. It didn't. Then, he ran his fingers over his sexy moustache and all I could do was imagine those same fingers on me, but I forced the thoughts aside and took a deep breath.

"Friends," he said.

"Yes. Friends. You've heard of those right?" I crossed my arms. "I'm a pretty decent one, I'm told."

He pushed out of the chair and moved toward me. I stepped back, grabbing for the edge of the bed when I tripped on the rug…not that I needed to. He caught me, which meant he also pulled me against him. The hand attached to the arm *not* holding me like a vice grip around my waist, slid to my neck and stroked my pulse, and he studied me, his eyes dropping to my mouth, which of course made them dry, so I just had to lick my lips. He smiled again. Damn it!

"What are you doing?" I demanded…okay, demand wasn't the word, because there was nothing demand-y about my voice. It was shaky and breathy…and might I add, somewhat turned on? God, I was insane!

"Do friends cut off other friends so they can't get a word in edgewise when trying to explain somethin' to the other one?" he asked.

"I wasn't—"

He raised an eyebrow. "Do friends jump to conclusions before askin' questions in order to understand a situation fully?"

"I didn't—"

"And tell me, Payton. What kind of friend is consumed twenty-four, seven with the desire to fuck the other one?"

Ohmigod! "I—"

His mouth landed on mine and I was transported somewhere so far out of the friend zone, it might as well have been the moon and this pissed me off, so I pushed at his shoulders and broke the kiss. I laid my fingers against my lips trying to ignore the tingle.

"In answer to your question, handsome. No, friends aren't consumed with the need to fuck each other," I snapped. "So maybe we can't be friends after all."

"Fuck me, Payton, what the hell do you want me to do?"

"I want you to stop kissing me every time you want to get your point across!"

"Damn it, woman!" He dragged his hands down his face. "You make me fuckin' crazy, you know that?"

I threw my hands up. "Bite me!"

His gaze swept my body from tip to toe and I shivered.

"Not literally," I rushed to say.

"Fuckin' shame, baby. I'd make it good for you."

"I hate you so much right now."

He sighed and his face softened. "I'm just askin' you to talk it out with me, Payton. Can you do that?"

"Honestly, Alex? I don't know. You're not what I expected. You're sure as hell nothing like anyone I've ever met, so I'm kind of lost as to what to do."

He smiled gently and held his hand out to me. "Break it down for me."

I took his hand and he led me back to the chairs. I sat in the one I'd been in before, and he did the same. I couldn't help looking over my shoulder and staring out at the view of the water. It was so incredibly calming and I needed that right now. "Relationships have always been easy for me," I admitted. "In the past, I've been friends with someone for a while, then we'd go on a few dates and decide if there was something to develop. If there was, we'd see each other for a period of time exclusively, then if we fell in love, we'd take it to the next level." I focused on Alex again. "There has never been drama. Ever. Even when the relationships didn't work out, we'd separate amicably and go on with our lives."

"Sounds pretty fuckin' borin', baby."

"Well, it wasn't. It was great," I countered. "I always knew where I stood, always understood where we were going. No guessing."

"Because it was all on your terms."

"It was not!"

"Babe, it was," he said. "Sounds like you dated a shit ton of pussies, none of them willing to fight for you or make you feel anything real. They let you run everything…afraid to disappoint the great Payton Williams."

I rolled my eyes. "You have no idea what you're talking about."

A Macey sounding giggle came from the hallway and I shot out of my seat to find my best friend with her hand over her mouth, standing about a foot from the open door.

"Eavesdropping now, Mace?" I snapped. "Nice."

"I was coming to find out if you still wanted to come with us or if we should go without you. I didn't mean to catch that last bit of the conversation," she said, and then raised her voice and added, "Even if he is totally right."

"He is *not* right! And, yes, I'm coming with you."

"Okay, well we need to get going."

I nodded. "Let's go."

"Give us a minute, babe," Alex said to Macey from right behind me. Again, I hadn't heard him move.

"Do you float?" I snapped.

"I'll give you a minute," Macey said, and walked away.

"I have to go," I said, and faced Alex.

He closed the bedroom door and stroked my cheek. "One minute."

I let out a frustrated sigh. "Fifty-eight seconds, handsome. Make 'em count."

"No one conspired against you, Payton. When I was at the club earlier, Booker did say Dani was joining you, but it was after you and I spoke and you said you were busy. He didn't say anything about Kim or driving them." He smiled. "I just wanted to see you, baby, and, yeah, I want to know you're safe. If I'm driving, then I can guarantee it."

I bit my lip. "You really didn't plan it?"

"Can't speak for the others, but no, I really didn't plan it."

I melted. "I still hate you."

He chuckled and ran his nose against mine. "No you don't."

"Yes I do," I whispered.

He kissed me gently. "No you don't."

I licked my lips. "Um, yeah, I do."

He grinned and kissed me again. "Um, no, you don't."

I wrinkled my nose, mostly because I didn't want to smile.

"I can keep doing this," he said.

"I bet you can."

Alex chuckled. "Forgive me?"

"For which part?" I retorted.

"All of it, baby. That way I'm covered."

I rolled my eyes. "I guess I should probably apologize too."

"What for? You're perfect, Payton."

"I never said I was perfect," I snapped.

"Don't get mad, baby." He smiled again. "I'm just fuckin' with ya. Don't get your panties in a wad."

"Don't tell me not to get my panties in a wad, then."

He raised an eyebrow. "We'll work on your sense of

humor."

"Bite…never mind."

Alex laughed and I couldn't help but smile.

"We friends?" he asked, and I punched his arm. "Shit, baby, that fuckin' hurt."

"Yeah, well, my brother taught me how to hit," I said smugly, but when I saw him rubbing his arm, I felt bad. "I didn't really hurt you, did I?" When he gave me an irritating smirk, I wanted to hit him again. "I'm back to hating you."

At that, he dropped his head back and let out a roar of a laugh. "Fuck me, baby, you're gorgeous."

"I'm going now," I said in a sing-songy voice, and pulled open the door.

Before I could step into the hallway, I was dragged up against Alex and kissed senseless. How was it possible kissing him just got better and better?

"Payton," Macey called, although, she was sounding a little less patient than before.

I pushed against Alex and he broke the kiss. "You're killing me," I complained.

"Told you I'd wear you down, baby."

"Come on," I said, and headed back to the living room. "Dallas and Brock left already?"

"Honey, you've been in there for like an hour," Macey said.

"Bite me, Mace." I heard Alex clear his throat behind me, but I didn't react. My body did though, and I had to take a few deep breaths to calm myself. "We ready?" I asked.

At the murmurs of assent, we locked up the apartment and headed to Mississippi Studios.

SIX

Payton

"**A**M I REALLY a control freak?" I asked Macey as we watched the rest of the group dancing on the floor a few feet in front of us.

She turned away from the dance floor and focused on me. "I have no idea what you're talking about."

I narrowed my eyes. "Mace."

"Okay. Let's just say, you're a bit of a hyper-administrative enthusiast, like me."

"I think I prefer 'outcome enthusiast.'"

Macey laughed. "Ohmigod, that's good."

"You really shouldn't be surprised by my brilliance." I shook my head. "But, be serious for a second."

"You're thinking about what Hawk said?"

I nodded.

"Okay." Macey sighed. "You know how people pretend to be afraid of me?"

"No one pretends, Mace."

Macey chuckled. "For the sake of argument, let's say they do pretend."

"Okay."

"Well, although people aren't typically afraid of you, they *do* want to live up to you."

I wrinkled my nose. "What?"

"You're an ideal, honey. People are drawn to you because you're beautiful and confident, and then they find out you have a wicked sense of humor and are sweet on top of that, and they can't help but want to be near you. But you expect the highest and best out of people and when they don't perform, you tend to back away a little."

My stomach churned a bit. "Why am *I* an ideal?"

"This is where I find you totally fascinating." Macey grinned. "On the outside, you appear to be perfect—" I opened my mouth to object, but she held up her hand. "I know, I know, you're not perfect. Just listen." I rolled my eyes, but I did close my mouth again. "Your family is amazing, you're amazing, even your pets have all been amazing."

We'd owned two dogs throughout our lives, a Boxer and a black lab. Our Boxer died when I was ten and our lab had died about three years ago. My parents couldn't bear to get another one, especially since us kids were all out of the house, so we were currently pet-less...unless you counted the stupid cat that showed up at the door and refused to leave. Probably because Mom fed it every day. But Macey was right. Our dogs had rocked. We'd taught them tricks, they never had to be leashed because we all worked with them, so yeah, they were pretty amazing.

"Your parents adore each other and have been married *forever*, you're actually *close* to your siblings, and you're all smart, educated, and other than you...although, that will happen, I know it...have married their soul mates. What isn't attractive about that?"

"But?" I said.

"*But*, and I say this not because there's anything wrong with you, just an observation."

"Yeah, yeah. Get to it, Mace."

"You have dated a *lot* of guys, honey. And other than Brendon and Curt, they've never lasted more than two or three months."

"Well, that's because I loved Bren and Curt."

"I know. I get it. But once you slept with them, you kind of went off them."

"What?" I gasped. "I did not."

"You waited to sleep with Curt for, what…nine months?"

I nodded.

"And your relationship lasted one year and two days, right?"

"Yes," I grumbled.

"And with Brendon you ultimately waited a year, honey. That's a long time for a guy to wait for something, especially when you'd already given him a little taste."

"Well, I needed to know if I loved him."

Macey squeezed my arm. "I'm not judging, honey. Just laying out the facts. You and Brendon lasted about two years, but in the end, you just weren't 'all that into him.' That man moved mountains to make you happy, which I personally think was part of the problem."

"What do you mean?"

"He got so wrapped up in everything Payton, he lost himself in the process. And that's on him, by the way, not you."

"So you're saying I'm kind of a bitch?"

"*No!*" she rushed to say. "Not at all. Neither of them fought for you. When you dumped them, they just went away, even though I know for a fact they were devastated. But if they loved you as much as they claimed, why wouldn't they fight? In the end, I just don't think either of those guys were your soul mate."

"And?"

"And I think Hawk might be."

"Shut up!"

Macey smiled. "He's known you for what, a week?"

"Yes."

"And he's figured you out, but not only that, he challenges you, which scares you."

"No, he terrifies me," I admitted.

"I know how you feel, honey. It was the same with me and Dallas. It's frightening when someone knows you so well, they can ruin you."

I chuckled. "Dallas would never ruin you."

"I know, but we've known each other for a really long time…it's far scarier when someone figures you out after a week. You don't know Hawk well enough yet to know if you can trust him."

"I can trust him," I said. I knew that I could, without a doubt.

Macey grinned.

"Oh, shut up," I grumbled.

"Just go with it," she said. "What's the worst that could happen?"

"I can think of a lot of things."

"If your heart gets broken, honey, you have a shit ton of people to put it back together. And if it doesn't and you find the love of your life, then you've gained everything."

She had a point.

"Ladies."

I glanced up to see two men standing at our table. One blond, one dark-haired, both bearded and very Portland hipster.

"Would either of you like to dance?" the blond one asked.

"No thanks," Macey said, and flashed her wedding finger.

"It's just a dance," he argued.

"No."

"What about you?" he asked me.

"Not much of a dancer, but thanks anyway."

"Come on," the dark-haired man slurred. "One dance."

Macey leveled both of them with a stare. "You sound drunk to me, and even if you weren't, I don't dance with anyone other than my husband, so I'd highly suggest you just walk away.”

The blond one scowled, but they did in fact walk away, and Macey and I went back to watching the other girls still out on the dance floor.

“I wish I liked to dance,” I admitted.

Macey chuckled. “Me too.”

“I have to pee. I’ll be right back,” I said, and pushed my chair away.

“You need me to come with?”

“No, I’m good. Just watch the table and my purse.”

Macey nodded and I headed for the ladies room. I was washing my hands when the bathroom door opened and I glanced in the mirror to find dark-haired hipster guy stepping inside.

I grabbed towels from the dispenser. “You got the ladies’, buddy. Guys’ is next door.”

He closed the door and locked it. “I know what I got.”

I faced him after throwing the paper towels into the garbage can. “Are you serious right now?”

On one hand, I’d had very little to drink, was pretty damn good at defending myself, and fought dirty. My brother taught me a lot. On the other, I was wearing four-inch heels, a little black dress, and my purse with my pepper spray was back at the table with Macey.

This made me annoyed more than nervous, so I crossed my arms and leaned against the sink. “What’s your plan, big guy?”

“I’m gonna get what I didn’t get earlier,” he slurred.

“You want to dance,” I droned.

He sneered. “I did before, but now I want something different.”

The doorknob jiggled and then banging at the door had the guy a little startled. “Busy in here!” he bellowed.

“Payton?” Alex called.

I frowned. He wasn’t here…or at least, I didn’t think he was. I’d told him I’d text him when he could pick me up.

“Give me a sec,” I yelled back, and then focused on the drunk. “That’s my very protective boyfriend out there, so you have a choice to make. Either you head on out the door, or you'll have to deal with me, *then* him."

I realized fleetingly that I'd just referred to Alex as my boyfriend, but being a little busy at the present time, I decided to process that later.

Alex banged on the door again. "Payton, I'm gonna fuckin' break down this door if you don't open it."

"I'm not really in a posi—"

I couldn't get another word out as the guy lunged at me. I shifted, managing to shove him, but his elbow came up and whacked me in the cheek as he went down…and it *hurt*, damn it. Before I could make it to the door, it slammed open and Alex forced his way inside, Booker behind him. Alex came to me immediately and pulled my hand away from my cheek. His face contorted with rage. "What'd he do?"

"He hit me on his way to the ground," I said, my eyes filling with tears from the pain.

"Okay, baby," he said, and kissed my forehead. "I'll take care of it."

Booker had his knee on the jerk's back and was shoving his head into the cold cement floor to keep him from moving. Drunk guy was squirming, but otherwise stuck where he was.

"Pay?" Macey peeked her head into the bathroom. "Ohmigod, what happened?"

"I'm okay," I said.

"Go with Macey, baby," Alex said, so I stepped around the man and into the hallway.

"Let me look," Macey demanded and she felt around the cheekbone. "Sorry, honey," she said when I grimaced. "I don't think anything's broken. Ice should help. I have an instant pack in my purse."

"Of course you do." I couldn't help but smile. She was an amazing nurse and always carried a mini first-aid kit wherever she went. How she fit an icepack in her clutch, I have no idea. "Ow," I breathed out. Smiling was apparently not the smart choice. The pained squeal of my would-be attacker brought my attention back to the bathroom and I gasped. Alex had the man on the ground, his hand wrapped around the hipster's neck.

"Alex, stop!" I demanded.

"Payton, get the fuck out of here," Alex snapped.

Macey grabbed my hand and tugged me away from the door.

"He's going to kill him," I said, and tried to pull my hand away.

"He's not going to kill him, honey," Macey said. "But you probably don't want to watch what he's more than likely going to do to him."

"I had everything under control," I argued.

"You can have that discussion later. Right now, Hawk needs to do what he needs to do."

My face was hurting from moving my mouth so I nodded and walked back to the table with Macey. She grabbed her purse, pulled out the little square icepack and squeezed it to activate the cooling magic, then placed it over my cheek.

Dani, Kim, and Bailey were laughing as they walked back to the table, but their expressions grew serious when they saw me.

"What happened?" Bailey asked as she sat next to me.

I filled them in and Dani shook her head. "Austin said nothing about staying, but I'm not surprised. I'm going to find him."

"I don't think that's a good idea," Macey countered. "They're in the middle of dealing with the asshole."

Dani sighed with a frown, but took her seat next to Kim.

* * *

Hawk

"You fuckin' touched my woman," I snapped as I dragged the asshole from the bathroom floor and slammed him against the wall. "Now you're gonna deal with me."

"I didn't mean to hit her, man, it was an accident."

Booker and I had stayed out of sight in order to keep an eye on Payton and Dani without them knowing we were there. I had watched the hipster douchebags stop at Payton's table and almost walked over then, but the men had walked away before I did, so I let things be.

I'd been watching Payton as she walked to the bathroom, thinking nothing of it until one of the guys that had been harassing her at the table walked in behind her and closed the door. I made my way to the door, found it locked, and knew something was off.

"What the fuck are you doing?"

Dragging me from my thoughts, I turned to the sound of the male voice and recognized the second of the table douchebags. "Your buddy attacked my woman."

"What the fuck, Noah?"

"I didn't attack her, Chris," Noah squealed. "It was an accident."

By now, the club manager had arrived, along with a couple of bouncers. Booker knew them, considering he ran *Blush*, so he dealt with them and the douchebag's friend while I took care of Noah.

"You're fuckin' hurtin' me, man," Noah complained.

I shoved him harder against the wall. "And what were you plannin' on doin' to my woman, asshole?"

"I just wanted to talk to her."

"You're a fuckin' liar," I snapped.

I forced myself not to kill the asshole, even though the second I'd seen Payton's face, I wanted to. It wouldn't work for me to go to jail.

"Mark's guys wanna handle him," Booker said after he'd stepped back into the bathroom.

"*I* wanna fuckin' handle him," I snapped.

"Let Mark's guys handle me," Noah squeaked.

If I hadn't been so pissed, I probably would have

laughed. After one more shove against the wall because I needed to inflict a little more pain, I let Noah go. "Fuckin' pussy. I ever see you near my woman again, I'll fuckin' kill you. Hear me?"

Noah nodded, and I released him. Mark ushered Noah out of the bathroom and I dragged my hands down my face.

Booker frowned. "Let's go outside, brother."

I studied him for a minute and then nodded. It wouldn't be a good idea for Payton to see me like this, and the fresh air might calm me down. Booker led me out the back door and I paced the alley. "Fuckin' bastard."

My phone buzzed in my pocket and I pulled it out and read the screen.

Payton: Headache from hell, would like to go now.

I frowned, my worry for her concerning. "Payton wants to go home."

"I can take Macey if you need some time," Booker offered.

"Payton's stayin' with her tonight, so I'll take 'em."

Booker nodded and headed toward the door.

I followed. "Thanks for havin' my back, brother."

Booker gave me a chin lift and then we headed back to the table.

* * *

Payton

The ice was warming and my cheek was throbbing, and a splintering pain was shooting through my head. To say I felt somewhat wrecked and pathetic was an understatement.

"You ready, baby?"

I glanced up to find Hawk holding his hand out to me, his face impassive, but his eyes anxious. I nodded and let him pull me to my feet. He didn't say anything as we headed to the truck, Macey following, but I could feel his edginess as he helped me into the truck and closed the door.

He drove us back to Macey's, still saying nothing. Macey

was also quiet, but probably because she was texting furiously behind me. I assumed she was filling Dallas in on the evening.

Alex drove into the garage and parked the truck. He glanced at me and then frowned.

"Why don't you come up, Hawk?" Macey said.

"You sure?" he asked.

"Yep. You guys need to talk."

"Thanks, babe." Hawk climbed out of the truck, helped Macey out, and then came to my side, pulling open the door.

I smiled, forcing myself not to grimace at the pain in my cheek. "Are you mad, Alex?"

He frowned. "Not at you."

"I'm okay."

"He fuckin' hit you, Payton."

I wanted to point out again that it had technically been an accident, but the fact he'd been in there for nefarious reasons to begin with, my argument didn't really make sense. Instead, I stroked Alex's cheek. "I know, but I'm okay."

He shook his head and wrapped his arms around me so he could lift me out of the truck. I settled my hands on his shoulders as he lowered me to the ground and he stared at me for a few seconds before scowling and slamming the truck door shut.

We followed Macey upstairs and into the apartment. Macey closed and locked the door behind us and smiled at me. "I'm going to call Dallas. There's beer in the fridge and you know where the wine is, Pay. Help yourself."

"Thanks, Mace."

She left the room and I set my purse on the kitchen island. "Beer?"

"Yeah, babe, thanks."

I grabbed a beer out of the fridge and Alex took it from me before I could open it. He twisted off the cap and took a swig. I opened the freezer and grabbed an icepack, then found Macey's stash of ibuprofen and took two.

Before I could lay the icepack against my cheek, Alex

hissed, "Fuck me."

"Is it really that bad?" I asked.

"Yeah, babe, it's pretty bad."

I stepped into the foyer and glanced in the mirror hanging on the wall. Yeah, that was gonna leave a mark. I sighed and settled the icepack against my cheek again. Alex was watching me as I walked back to the living room, his body locked, his expression one of concern…no, not concern. Rage.

I gave him a little smile and his expression softened as he held his arm out to me. I slid into his embrace and wrapped the arm I wasn't using to hold the ice around his waist.

"I wanted to kill him."

"I'm picking up on that," I said.

He stroked my healthy cheek and then kissed me gently. I smiled against his lips. "As much as I want to stand here and keep doing this, my feet are killing me. I have to get these shoes off."

Alex nodded and I flopped onto the sofa. As I leaned down to take care of the shoes, he knelt on the floor and did it for me, guiding my feet to his lap after he'd sat next to me. We sat in silence for several minutes as he massaged my feet. By the time the icepack had warmed, my eyes were drooping and I was biting back several yawns.

"I should probably go," he said.

I nodded, but had to admit my heart was a little broken. I didn't want him to leave.

"What time do you want me to pick you up tomorrow?"

"I don't have anything planned, but if it's before ten, you may die."

He chuckled. "Noted."

I slid my feet from his lap and stood, dropping the icepack on the coffee table. Alex was quiet as I walked him to the door, but he kissed me so I didn't much care.

"Club get together tomorrow night. Wanna come?" he asked after breaking the kiss.

I smiled. "With you?"

Alex raised an eyebrow. "Yeah with me."

"Possibly. I'd like to see how bad this looks before I venture into a social setting." Rage crossed his face again and I laid a hand on his chest. "Sorry."

"I might still kill him."

"Not that I'm complaining, but what were you doing there to begin with?" I asked. "I thought you were leaving the club?"

"Never said that, babe."

"You kind of implied it when you dropped us off and said to text you when we were ready and then you drove away," I countered.

"Yeah. I parked. Then I came in, sat with Booker, and waited." He slipped his hand to my neck and squeezed. "If I hadn't been there…"

"I could have handled it."

"He fuckin' hit you, Payton!" he snapped.

"That part was an accident, honey. It happened when he was on his way to the ground. My brother and Dallas have taught me and Macey to defend ourselves, and the guy was so drunk, he could barely stand."

He frowned. "Fucker."

"Yes. Definitely." I smiled. "But I really was okay. Not that I totally don't appreciate you breaking in all bad ass and such."

"Bad ass and such?" Now he smiled and I melted. A hard-won smile from Alex 'Hawk' James was better than anything on the planet…at least what I'd experienced so far.

I chuckled. "You're kind of sexy when you're defending my honor."

"There's a spare bedroom here, right?"

"Yes." I wanted nothing more, but I bit my lip and shook my head. "But, no."

He chuckled. "Okay, baby. Reprieve for now. Get some sleep and I'll call you tomorrow."

I grinned up at him. "Call me when you get home."

"Greedy."

I nodded and his mouth covered mine for the best good-night kiss I'd ever received. I wished to God Macey wasn't in the apartment right then, because I would have dragged him back to the spare room and showed him just how greedy I was.

SEVEN

Payton

THANKSGIVING MORNING I woke up excited. I hadn't seen Alex since the morning after girls' night out when he informed me he had "club business," so we couldn't hang out, so he dropped me home, kissed me quickly, and was gone. To make matters worse, the week got away from us, and we'd only managed a few stolen moments on the phone. The only bright spot on our drive home was that Lily was with him, so she and I got to talk a little and I convinced Alex to stop at Starbucks for hot chocolates which helped me butter up his daughter.

I showered and did my makeup and hair, but dressed in sweats and a T-shirt first, since I knew we'd be doing last minute cleaning and I didn't want to sweat through everything. I walked upstairs to find the house in organized chaos, Bailey and my sisters were already in the kitchen, Brock and my brothers-in-law more than likely hiding. Macey and Dallas would be here later, which was surprising. It was rare

Brock and Dallas had holiday time off at the same time.

"Good morning, sunshine. Nice of you to show," my oldest sister Kristen droned sarcastically.

I stuck my tongue out at her before I pulled her in for an extra long, annoyingly sappy hug. I was a hugger…Kris, not so much.

Bailey chuckled. "I just got here five minutes ago, so you're in good company."

"Where are Mom and Dad?" I asked and hugged my other older sister, Anna.

"Herding the kids," Anna said. "Or having sex in a closet."

"Ew! Anna!" Kristen complained. "Gross."

"Talk to Dad about it. He overshares."

"He told you they were going to have sex in a closet?" Bailey asked.

"He calls Mom his GILF. He implies it every time he says it."

"Okay, enough of that subject," I said with a laugh. "What can I do to help?"

"Mom bought stuff for the kids and put them on the table. Mugs or something," Anna said. "Can you grab the candy and fill them, please?"

"No problem." I grabbed the bags of chocolates from the hiding place in the pantry and headed to the large dining room table.

My mom had purchased Christmas mugs for each of the little kids, including one for Lily, which would also be used to mark their place settings at the kids' table. Thinking of Lily brought Alex to mind and my stomach fluttered. I couldn't wait to see him…and kiss him. That made me think again about Lily and now my heart dropped. I wouldn't be able to kiss him. His daughter would be with him…and his sister.

"Why so glum?"

I raised my head to see my brother walking toward me.

"I'm not glum."

"You're in your head, sissy, I can tell." Brock sat in the chair at the head of the table to my left. "Thinking about Hawk?"

I sighed. "Yeah."

"He's a pretty good guy, Pay."

"You think?"

"Yeah." He smiled. "He's clean."

"Ohmigod, Brock. You did a background check on him?"

"Are you surprised?"

I rolled my eyes. "No, I guess not, but it would have been nice to know beforehand."

"You know me. I want to know what I'm up against."

"*You?*" I paused in the doling out of candy. "You have nothing to do with this."

He rose to his feet and gave me a mock clip of the chin. "Oh, Payton, you are so cute."

"Bite me, Brock."

"Payton!" my mother snapped. "Language."

Where the hell she'd come from, I have no idea.

"Yeah, Payton, watch your fuckin' *language*," Brock whispered, and gave me a smug smile.

"Don't fall asleep, big brother. Ever," I threatened.

He laughed and left me to my work as my mother walked into the dining room.

"Morning, honey," she said, and kissed my cheek.

"Hi, Mom. Kids settled?"

"Yep. Best investment in our whole life is that big screen television. However, it's *Frozen* again." She grinned and sat where Brock had been earlier. "I just couldn't stick around, so Elizabeth is keeping an eye on things."

I chuckled. Elizabeth was the oldest niece, Kristen's daughter, and she was great with the littler kids.

"So," my mom said, and laid her hand on my arm.

"So."

"Tell me about this man."

I had a feeling this was coming, and my mom and I were super close, but she still managed to relegate me to a teenager on occasion. "Not sure what to say. He's nice."

"Single dad."

I sighed. "Yeah. He's a single dad."

"And what's his ex-wife like?"

"He was never married. She took off when Lily was little, so he hasn't seen her in years. Doesn't even know where she is."

"Wow. So, he's responsible."

I smiled. "Yeah, Mom, he's responsible."

"Did your brother do his thing?"

"Yes, Mom. Alex is a 'good guy' according to Brock."

Mom chuckled. "Well, your dad got a good vibe off him."

"Vibe, Mom, really?"

"What? It's the perfect word in this situation."

"I like him," I said, and then gasped.

"What?"

"I forgot to tell him we dress up."

"Oh, honey, don't worry about it. We don't care what he's wearing."

"I know, but I don't want him to feel weird." I bit my lip. "But then again, he probably doesn't care. He's kind of his own man."

"The perfect kind." My mom rose to her feet. "I'm going to check on the food."

"I'll be in when I'm done."

"Sounds good."

My mom left and I grabbed my phone, debating if I should call Alex or not. They wouldn't be arriving for a couple of hours, but if I told him to dress up, I felt like I was trying to change him somehow. I slipped my phone back into my pocket. I liked him just the way he was, so I'd take him however he came. Done with the mugs, I headed to the kitchen to help with the rest of the prep.

* * *

Hawk

I was helping Lily with her tights when my phone buzzed in my pocket. "Just a second, baby girl." I grabbed my phone and frowned. I didn't recognize the number, but answered it anyway. "Yo."

"Hawk?"

"Yeah."

"Hey, baby. It's Jenny."

My blood ran cold. I laid my hand over the speaker and called, "Kayla?"

"Yeah?"

"Can you come help Lily?"

My sister appeared in the doorway. At first, she looked pissed, but then she raised an eyebrow.

"Jenny," I whispered.

"What the hell does she want?"

I shrugged and walked out of the room, leaving Kayla to take care of Lily, while I closed myself into my bedroom.

"What the fuck do you want?" I bit out.

"Come on, baby. Don't be like that. We have a baby together."

"*We* don't have shit together, Jenny. *I* have a little girl who knows nothing about you and never will because you walked out on her."

"I just want to see her. See how she is."

I forced myself not to break something. "Never gonna happen."

"I'm doin' real good, baby. Been clean for nine months."

"You're on drugs now?"

"No. That's what I'm sayin'. I'm clean. I was in a bad way for a couple a years. But I'm good now."

"Jenny, you weren't usin' when you left, so what the fuck

81

changed?”

“I was young, Hawk. Stupid.”

“You were *thirty*!”

“Look, I didn’t call to fight. I want to see Lily. I’m back in the area and I have the right to see my daughter.”

“No fuckin’ way.”

“Don’t make me get a lawyer.”

“Jenny, do whatever the fuck you need to do. I gotta go.” I hung up and sat on the edge of the bed, dropping my face into my hands. A knock at my door brought me out of my head and I sighed. “Come in.”

Kayla sat beside me and frowned. “What did she want?”

“She wants to see Lily.”

“Why?”

I filled my sister in on the conversation which was probably a mistake. Kayla hated Jenny even more than I did, so the news wound her up tight.

“Fuckin’ bitch,” Kayla snapped. “No, she’s a cunt.”

“Yeah, but I don’t want to think about Jenny,” I said. “Right now, I need to see Payton. It’s been almost a week and I fuckin’ miss her.”

This brought a smile to Kayla’s face. “You really like her.”

“Ya think?”

“You’ve never acted like this before and you know it.”

“Yeah. I guess you’re right.” I groaned.

“What?”

“I love her, Kay.”

My sister gasped. “Seriously?”

I nodded. “She’s everything I never knew I wanted—”

“Or thought you deserved,” she interrupted.

“I don’t fuckin’ deserve her and the thought of losin’ her…” I couldn’t finish the thought.

“Hey. You’re not going to lose her. I’ll help however I can.”

I smiled. “I know, babe. Couldn’t do life without you.

Don't know if I've told you how much I appreciate you, but I'm telling you now."

Kayla grinned. "Back atya."

I sighed. "This shit with Jenny is the worst fuckin' timin'."

"Well, in general, yeah, but why, specifically?"

"Payton doesn't do drama."

"She's a woman, how the hell does she avoid drama?" Kayla asked.

I laughed. "Yeah, but bitch drama? Not sure she'll put up with it."

Kayla patted my knee. "If it's meant to be, it'll be."

"You dump your asshole of an old man and now you're a sage."

She wagged a finger at me. "Don't you forget it."

"Daddy." Lily ran into the room. "I put my soos on."

I glanced at her feet. "You did a great job, baby girl, but they're on the wrong feet."

She lowered her head, then smiled and crossed one foot over the other. "Not anymore."

I laughed and scooped her up, holding her above my head. "Do you know how much I love you?"

"All the way to the moon," she squealed.

I lowered her enough so she could wrap her arms around my neck and her legs around my waist. "I love you, Daddy."

"Love you too, baby girl. Let's fix those shoes and then we'll go hang out with Payton."

"Yay," she sang.

Setting her on the ground, I fixed her shoes, and then we headed to Vancouver.

* * *

Payton

Because I had no idea what Alex would be wearing, I chose to dress down a little. I wore a dark pair of jeans, a festive red sweater with a deep V-neck and a black lace cami underneath it. My knee-high black boots finished off the outfit and because they were my favorite, I felt extra comfortable.

I was standing in the kitchen when I heard the doorbell ring. Since Macey and Dallas had arrived thirty minutes ago, I knew it had to be Alex. "I'll get it."

I rushed to the foyer, my heart racing in anticipation. I smoothed my hands over my jeans and then pulled open the door, my breath leaving my body. I didn't think Alex could get better looking, but he wore dark jeans, almost black, a dark blue button up shirt, open at the throat, and a pair of black boots that looked in better shape than his regular motorcycle boots. I smiled. "Hi."

"Hey, baby," he whispered, his eyes raking over me. "This is my sister, Kayla."

Kayla looked a lot like her brother. And I mean, a *lot*. I looked a little like my siblings, but mostly like Brock, so people figured out we were related, but Kayla was the feminine version of Alex and she was beautiful. Long blonde hair, the same blue eyes as her brother, and she was tall and slim…model slim. Her hair was bigger than I was used to and her makeup was heavier, but she was gorgeous. I shook her hand and smiled. "Nice to meet you, hon," Kayla said.

"You too."

"Hi, Payton," Lily said, unable to stand still.

"Hi." I hunkered down in front of her. "You look beautiful, sweetheart."

She wore a red dress with black tights and black sparkly shoes. Her blonde hair had been pulled back at the sides and curled, and she wore pink lip-gloss.

"Fank you," she said.

"My nieces are all downstairs and you know what they're doing?"

"What?"

"They're watching *Frozen.*"

Her eyes got wide. "They *awa*?"

I nodded. "Do you want to join them?"

She looked up at her father. "Can I, Daddy?"

"Let's meet everyone and then, yes, baby girl, you can."

Lily jumped up and down. "'Kay, Daddy."

I rose to my feet. "Come on in and I'll introduce you to the masses."

They stepped inside and Alex's hand brushed my back before I led them into the great room where all of the adults were congregated. I was grateful my family hadn't followed me to the door, but now, they stared at Alex in open interest.

"Everyone, this is Alex, Kayla, and Lily," I said, and the group rose enmasse, and the next few minutes were spent with introductions.

I was glad Alex at least knew Brock and Dallas. I was confident they would make him feel included. I was a little concerned about Kayla, but then Kristen and Bailey descended on her, commenting on how beautiful she was, and Kayla was returning the compliments, so it appeared she was well in hand.

"I'm just going to show Lily where the other kids are," I said.

Lily grabbed onto Hawk's leg, but he knelt beside her and pulled her close. "I'm coming baby girl. I'm not going anywhere."

"Okay, Daddy," she said, and he rose to his feet.

Lily slipped her tiny hand into his big one and Alex smiled at me. "She's good."

I nodded and led them to the basement stairs. We arrived at the double doors just as "the song" started and I heard the voices of Elizabeth and Molly singing at the top of their lungs. I watched Lily's face brighten as we walked into the entertainment room. Billy, my seven-year-old nephew (and Molly's brother) was in the corner, headphones on and his face stuck in a gaming device. The baby, Callie who was two, was doing her best to keep up with her sister and cousin, a big grin on her chubby face as she bobbed to the music.

I grabbed the remote and paused the television, my nieces turning in annoyance to face me. "I want you to meet Lily. Lily, this is Elizabeth and Molly."

Elizabeth grinned and made her way to Lily. "Hi Lily. Do you want to watch *Frozen* with us?"

Lily nodded and looked up at Alex.

"I think Lily wants to know her Dad is close," I said.

"If you want to see your dad, I'll take you okay?" Elizabeth said. "You just let me know."

Lily released Alex's hand and rushed to my niece. I gave Elizabeth the remote with a grin. "You're the bomb."

Elizabeth chuckled. "I know, Auntie, I know."

Alex and I watched the girls for a few minutes, but since Lily appeared totally comfortable, we took the distraction to leave the game room. I led Alex back toward the stairs, but found myself pulled into the room closest to the stairs. The room was my mother's craft room and typically a mess, which meant the door was usually closed. But for whatever reason, it was open and I found myself pushed against the wall and kissed almost to the point of no return.

"Fuck, baby," Alex whispered, dropping his forehead to mine once he broke the kiss. "I have missed you."

"You have?"

"Yeah." He stroked my pulse.

"Me too," I rasped. "You have no idea."

"I think I do." He smiled. "You look incredible."

"Thank you. So do you." I licked my lips. "I kind of want to peel you out of those jeans."

"Do it."

I squeezed my eyes shut. "You're killing me."

"Would now be the wrong time to point out you're the one making us wait?"

I glared up at him. "Yes, it absolutely would."

Alex grinned. "We'll have our time."

"I'm really looking forward to it."

"Fuck me," he whispered.

"Yes, please."

He groaned. "Payton."

"Sorry," I said. "Not helping."

"No, not helping at all." He kissed me again. "You really are beautiful, baby."

"Thank you."

"How's your bruise?"

"Much better. I put a little makeup over it."

He narrowed his eyes. "I see that."

I laid my hands on his chest. "We should get back upstairs."

"In a minute."

"I'm really glad you're here."

"Me too." He took my hand and kissed my palm.

"Did you get everything done this week?"

He nodded. "Everything I could. As long as someone doesn't jump bail this weekend, I might have the next few days off."

"Is there like a numbering system? Someone else might get called up before you?"

Alex shrugged. "Depends on who jumps bail. I offer a certain set of skills others don't."

"Oh," I said. "Probably won't ask what."

"Probably a good idea."

"We should go back up."

He nodded.

I licked my lips. "But I need another kiss."

He chuckled and obliged.

Arriving back upstairs, Kayla and Kristen had their heads together and were staring at a recipe card.

"She fits right in," I said, and smiled up at Alex.

He laid his hand on my lower back and nodded. "She does that."

"Hawk," Dallas called, and headed our way. "Guys are on the deck. As is the beer."

Alex chuckled. "Say no more."

I frowned up at him. "What? You don't want to help us make the pies?"

"There is nothing more I'd love to do, baby, but I'm thinkin' it's better I don't burn down your house."

"You're so full of crap." I chuckled. "Go play with the boys."

He grinned and followed Dallas outside. I made my way to the kitchen and joined Macey at the back counter rolling out dough. "Remind me why your mom insists on doing it this way? We could just buy pie crust."

I bumped her hip with mine. "She's a purist. And admit it, you love her pies."

Macey sighed. "I do love her pies. Of course, I don't see her here *making* said pies."

"Never said she was a dumb purist."

Macey grinned.

"What time are your grandparents coming?" I asked, and sprinkled flour on the rolling mat.

Macey had lost both her parents when she was young and had essentially been raised by her grandparents, with a lot of help from my parents. Macey was simply another sister in the sea of all my family adopted.

"In about an hour." She rolled over the dough, then again. "I told Gran not to bring anything, but she probably won't listen. She still insists on doing too much."

"You can't stop her and I personally love almost everything she cooks," I said. "Let's just hope she brings something other than pie."

Macey laughed. "Amen to that."

We managed to finish up the pies relatively quickly before my mom arrived to commandeer the kitchen. Macey and I were released so we headed out onto the deck to find our men. Alex grinned when he saw me, pushing away from the deck railing. He'd put on his dark brown leather jacket again and I wrapped my arms around him and squeezed.

"Didn't realize it was so cold out here."

"Where's your jacket?"

"Inside." I smiled up at him. "You'll do in a pinch."

He chuckled and slid his arm around my waist.

My mom peeked out of the French doors with a smile. "Chuck, honey. Bird's ready to be carved. If the rest of you want to get the kids washed up and seated, we're about to eat."

I walked Alex back inside and took his jacket before making our way downstairs to retrieve Lily. Kayla and Kristen were helping my mom with the food, so I was free to help with the kids.

Dinner was amazing. I don't know why, but I was a little surprised (happily, of course) at how well Alex, Kayla, and Lily fit into my family. Lily was totally relaxed with the rest of the kids, even helping with Callie in the highchair. I was falling in love with her almost as quickly as I was with her dad.

The dinner dishes cleared and dessert served, Kristen's husband Gordon tapped his glass with a knife and rose to his feet. "Kris and I have an announcement."

Alex's hand settled on my thigh and I linked my fingers with his.

"We're pregnant."

We all let out a cry of joy and I saw that Anna's eyes filled with tears almost as quickly as mine. It had taken my sister about a month to get pregnant with Elizabeth and then had several miscarriages and secondary infertility issues. They had pretty much given up thinking they'd ever have a second child.

I jumped to my feet and wrapped my arms gently around her, followed by the rest of the family.

"We're optimistically hopeful," Gordon continued. "She's twenty weeks and the doctors say everything looks good. It's a boy."

More celebration happened, then we finished dessert, did

dishes, still in celebratory mode, before congregating in the entertainment room for a family movie and egg nog. As I sat on one side of Alex, Lily on the other, pulled up against his chest, I couldn't imagine a better moment in my life to date. I had my family and my man close and it was perfect.

EIGHT

Payton

THE SATURDAY AFTER Thanksgiving, Alex was picking me up to take me to a club get-together and I was a little nervous. Our status had changed since the last time I was there and according to Macey who'd heard it from Dani, it was a big deal. I was just glad Dani would be there tonight, considering Dallas was home, so I'd lost my backup.

Alex had suggested I pack a change of clothes in case it got late and we decided to stay at the club. He'd quickly followed up that statement with a promise that nothing would happen if I didn't want it to. I smiled. Something was most definitely going to happen if I had any say in it.

I took care with my appearance, although, I dressed a little more casually than I normally did. I wore the same dark pair of jeans I'd worn at Thanksgiving, my knee-high boots, and a long-sleeved Harley Davidson T-shirt that Macey and I found the previous week. It was black, tight-fitting, and made my B's look like C's. It rocked.

My parents were at Kristen's house for dinner, so I let them know not to wait up, and grabbed my jacket, bag, and purse, dropping them by the front door. The weather had been unusually warm all day, but I knew that couldn't possibly last, so I'd packed a sweatshirt in case.

Sexy undies, check. Toothbrush, check. Change of clothes, check.

Yep, I was ready. And nervous.

Crap! I was nervous. I didn't get nervous, typically. I mean, tonight was a big night. I jumped when the doorbell rang, probably because I was standing directly underneath the bell part of it in the hallway, but I took a deep breath and made my way to the door, pulling it open.

Alex stood before me in jeans, boots and a leather jacket, and he was *hot*. Like, ohmigod, I have to squeeze my legs together hot. He was also alone.

"Hi," I breathed.

"Hey baby." He leaned down to kiss me and I was very tempted to drag him into the house and strip him naked. Unfortunately, he broke the kiss sooner that I would have liked. "Missed that."

"Me too." I smiled up at him. "Where's Lily?"

"Kayla's got her. You got a leather jacket?"

I nodded. "Yes. Why?"

"You're on my bike."

"Ah…okay."

"You'll be fine."

"I'm not nervous. Dallas has taken me out a few times. I guess I'm just surprised you're riding in this weather."

"It's perfect today and it's important."

"Come in, honey, I'll find my jacket." I stepped back and waited for him to enter before closing the door behind him. "Why's riding important?" I asked as I opened the door to the coat closet. He didn't answer, so I leaned around the door. He was watching me, his eyes reflective. "Alex?"

"Find your coat, baby, and we'll talk."

"You okay?"

He nodded. "Find your coat."

I stepped into the closet with a frown and rifled through the copious amounts of outerwear my parents kept jammed inside.

I found the black leather jacket that my brother bought me back when Dallas had first taken me out on his Harley. I hadn't worn it in a really long time, so I had no idea if it still fit.

I closed the door and made my way back to Alex. He looked concerned, which I didn't like on any level. "You're kind of freaking me out a bit."

"I love you."

I gasped. "I'm sorry?"

"I love you, Payton."

I bit my lip. "Why do you look like you're going to puke?"

"Sorry." He dragged his hands through his hair. "I've never said that to anyone before."

"Alex?" I whispered, laying my hands on his chest.

He smiled down at me. "Yeah, baby."

I stared up at him for a few seconds, taking stock of my feelings. I'd never felt this way about anyone, even the exes I'd claimed to love. What I felt for Alex well surpassed my feelings for Brendon and Curt. Alex was everything to me. Even in such a short amount of time, he meant more to me than anyone I'd ever known. "I love you too."

I didn't have time to notice his expression because his lips were suddenly on mine and I was lifted off my feet. Still in the air, I broke the kiss and dropped my forehead to his. "Will you do something for me?"

"Anything, baby."

"Will you take me somewhere private where you can take your time?"

He hissed through his teeth. "I'm taking you to the boat.

Now."

I chuckled. "I wasn't saying it had to be now."

He lowered me to the floor again. "If Kayla can take Lily home, we'll go later."

"Yeah?"

"Yeah."

I clapped my hands. "Let's go," I said. Alex laughed and grabbed my bag, and I followed him out the door. "Oh, wait! Helmet."

"I brought one," he said.

"No, it's okay. I have one. It's in the garage." I ran back inside and into the garage, grabbing the helmet my brother had bought me with the leather jacket. I set the alarm and locked up, joining Alex at his bike.

"No way in hell are you wearin' that, Payton."

"What? Why not? It fits perfectly and it's brother approved."

"It's pink paisley."

"I know." I grinned. "He was pranking Dallas, but it works fine and it's super cute."

"You got your car keys?"

I nodded and he held his hand out for them. I dug in my purse while he held my helmet and handed the keys to him, which he promptly took, popped the trunk and dropped my helmet into it. "What are you doing?" I demanded.

He smiled and threw my bag and purse (once he'd put the keys back in it) into his saddle bags…the hard kind that were more like tiny little trunks on the side…and then handed me a black helmet that was nowhere *near* as cool as mine. "Really?" I droned sarcastically.

Alex nodded. "It's Kayla's. It'll fit."

"But mine's so pretty."

He cupped my neck and gave it a gentle squeeze. "Don't need a pretty helmet when you make everything beautiful just by existing, baby."

I dropped my head back and laughed. "Ohmigod, honey,

you're good."

"You'll see just how good in a few hours." I shivered and he leaned down to kiss me, breaking the connection faster than I would have liked. "Hold that thought."

I nodded and pulled on my helmet. He did the same, climbing on the bike and waiting for me to join him.

The ride into Portland was gorgeous. The sun wouldn't set for another hour, and it shone off the Columbia as we headed over the bridge. We pulled into the parking lot of Big Ernie's Body Shop (the front this time) and Alex maneuvered the bike into the end space next to other just as gorgeous Harleys. He lowered the kickstand and waited for me to climb off the bike before doing the same.

I pulled off my helmet, hoping my hair wasn't completely wrecked, and Alex took it from me after grabbing my purse from one of the saddlebags.

He leaned down and kissed me quickly before stroking my cheek. "Tonight's different."

"It's not a get together?"

Alex smiled. "No, it is, but you're here on my bike, so everyone inside knows you're mine."

Understanding dawned and I looked up at him. "Oh."

"Yeah, oh." He kissed me again. "Mine."

I nodded. "Yours, but that also means *you* are *mine*."

He chuckled. "Yeah, Payton. I'm yours."

"So long as that's clear."

"God, I love you," he whispered on a chuckle.

"Kinda love you too, honey."

He took my hand, kissed my palm, and then led me to an unmarked door to the left of what looked like the actual shop. A dimly lit hallway led to another unmarked door which opened before we reached it. Alex pulled me into a small foyer with a few easy chairs and a desk with television sat in the space.

"Payton! Daddy!" Lily squealed, and a flurry of blonde flew at her father.

Alex scooped her up and hugged her. "Hey, baby girl. Are you having fun?"

"Kayla bought me *Fwozen*!"

"Did she now?" Alex looked at me with mock horror.

I saw Kayla walking towards us, a look of smug contrition on her face. "Payton started it."

I chuckled. "It's my fault now?"

Lily reached for me and I took her from Alex. "Hey, honey. How are you?"

She took my face in her hands. "Can I come to your house, pweese?"

"Not tonight, but another time, absolutely. You're always welcome there."

Lily hugged my neck and I melted. I mean, really, was there anything sweeter?

"How about we go back to the playroom," Kayla said.

"I want Payton."

I grinned. "What if you show me? Then I can meet your friends before I hang out with your daddy for a little while."

Lily smiled. "'Kay."

I lowered her to the floor and she grabbed my hand, tugging me toward the door to the common room. "Wait, honey. Let me talk to your dad real quick." I led her back to Kayla and Alex. "Is there anything I need to know?"

Alex chuckled. "No, babe. You're good."

I narrowed my eyes for a few seconds and then nodded. "Okay, honey," I said to Lily. "I'm ready."

She led me into the common room and then to a hallway at the back of the kitchen. The doorknob to the playroom was a little difficult to turn for her little hand, so I did it for her and pushed the door open.

"Will you dance wiff me, Payton?"

I cringed internally, but smiled at Lily. "I'd *love* to dance with you, honey."

One of the other women in the room smiled at me and Lily. "Hey, baby."

"Hi Sawwy."

The woman had red hair, big…Texas big, really heavy makeup, and wore leather pants, a tight long-sleeved T-shirt and a leather vest with 'Property of Flinch' on a patch on the front. "I'm Sally."

"Hi." I shook her hand. "I'm Payton. It's nice to meet you."

Lily ran to the bookcase that housed the DVDs and grabbed the *Frozen* cover.

"You Hawk's woman?" Sally asked, quietly which I appreciated.

"Yeah, it's looking that way." I smiled. "We're taking it slow for Lily."

"I hear that."

I spent a few minutes chatting with Sally before Lily commandeered me again and I danced a little with her to "the song," Sally joining in on the fun. Sally gave me a nod and then distracted Lily so I could sneak out.

I pushed open the door to find myself pulled into Alex's arms and kissed quite thoroughly. I smiled against his lips and broke the kiss. "Hi."

"Hey, baby. Missed you."

I chuckled. "It's barely been half an hour."

He drew his eyebrows together. "And?"

"Are you getting all gooey on me?"

Alex laughed. "Fuckin' kill me if I do."

I shook my head. "I kind of like the softer side of you."

"You do?" He slid his hand to my neck and stroked my pulse.

"Yes. Like the way you are with Lily." I wrapped my arms around his waist. "It's sexy."

"Right now, I want to take you up to my room."

I smiled up at him. "Yeah?"

"Yeah."

I licked my lips. "Let's go."

"Fuck, seriously?"

"Yes."

He grabbed my hand and led me out of the kitchen, through the common room, nodding occasionally at someone who called his name, but never pausing or stopping to talk. My man was on a mission and I was his goal.

We walked down a long hallway, up two flights of stairs, and then he unlocked the first door on the right. He pushed it open and stood back for me to precede him inside. He switched on the light before closing and locking the door behind him. I had no time to take in the room as Alex wrapped his arms around me and kissed me, guiding me to the bed and lifting me onto the mattress. He helped me remove my boots and socks, then kicked his off before leaning down and kissing me again. I slipped my hands under his shirt, the feel of his rock hard abs heady to the touch.

His lips moved to my neck, while a hand went to the hem of my shirt and pulled it off in one quick swoop. He pulled one bra cup down, scraping a nail across my nipple before leaning down to draw my nipple into his mouth. I gasped as he blew gently where he'd sucked, feeling the bud tighten as he sucked again.

I tugged at his shirt. "Off."

He straightened and slid off his cut, then reached behind him, pulling the long-sleeved T-shirt over his head. I hummed in delight at the sight of his chest. Dark blond hair spanned his pecs, while his stomach was somewhat bare. I loved that he didn't shave or wax all the way…it seemed more manly to me, plus it was soft to the touch and I couldn't wait to feel more.

He had tattoos, but he wasn't tatted out like I had expected from a biker. He had the Dogs of Fire logo on his inner forearm, and that same arm was sleeved up to his shoulder. The other arm was also sleeved, but ended at the elbow. Down his left side and slightly across his ribs was a black and white tattoo of the lily flower with the word "Lily" interwoven in the design.

I felt the clasp of my bra give and then Alex slid it down my arms. "Gorgeous, baby," he whispered as he cupped each breast and kissed me again. He pushed me onto my back and stretched out beside me, pulling me to him, my nipples hardening as my breasts connected with his chest.

My hand went to the waistband of his jeans and I unbuttoned the top and slid the zipper down, feeling his hard length against my hand. I slipped my hand under his boxer briefs to cup him, surprised by his size. He was bigger than I was used to, but for whatever reason, that excited me and I wrapped my hand around him and squeezed gently.

"Babe, hold on a second. If you keep doing that, I'm not gonna last."

"Sorry."

"Don't be sorry, baby. There's no rush." He kissed me quickly as he pushed my jeans and panties from my hips. I lost all coherent thought after that as he slid his hand between my legs and grinned. "Fuckin' wet."

I nodded and then gasped and he dragged my wetness to my clit with his finger. He slid from the bed and stood before me, staring down at me with a smile. He pushed open my knees, sliding my thighs over his shoulders and began a delicious assault on my pussy. I whimpered as he sucked, licked, and kissed every inch of my center. He slid one finger inside of me, and then two, and as much as I tried to make the sensations last, it was useless. I cried out as my orgasm hit and he released my shaking legs and climbed back onto the bed next to me. I tried to catch my breath as I licked my lips and turned to look at him. "I really *really* liked that."

"We're not done," he promised.

"Good," I said. "You're unbelievably beautiful, Alex."

"Back atya, baby." He grinned. "I love you."

I stroked his check. "I love you too, honey."

He leaned forward to kiss me, but a bang on the door had him scowling. "What the fuck?"

"Need to get downstairs, Hawk," Booker called. "Now!"

I sat up as Alex grabbed his shirt and tugged it on. "Don't move."

I nodded, but pulled his comforter around me while he headed for the door. As the bedding shifted, I heard metal on metal and lifted the pillow to see a pair of handcuffs secured to one of the iron railings in the headboard. I didn't have time to process what I was seeing due to the fact Alex stormed back inside and grabbed my discarded clothing off the floor. "Get dressed."

"What's wrong?"

"Just get dressed, Payton," he snapped, and pulled on his boots and cut.

I nodded and slid from the bed, suddenly self-conscious about my nudity. Alex waited until I'd pulled on my boots and smoothed my hair (sort of) before pulling open the door again and waving me out of the room. Booker paced the hallway but fell beside Alex as we made our way back downstairs.

"Who the fuck let her in?" Alex asked Booker.

"Susie," Booker said. "Prez's pissed."

"Fuck me."

I didn't know who Susie or Prez were, or why Prez was pissed, but I knew that whoever was here was not welcomed by Alex. As we hit the common room, I was suddenly flanked by Dani and Kayla.

"What's going on?" I whispered.

Dani wrapped her arms around my shoulders and gave me a gentle squeeze. "Lily's mom—"

"That bitch is no one's mother, Dani. Fuckin' egg donor is all she's good for," Kayla corrected.

"Where's Lily?" I asked.

"Sally's got her hidden upstairs. They're watchin' a movie," Kayla said.

I nodded and focused on Alex. His body was stiff and unyielding as he crossed his arms and stared at a woman standing in the middle of the room. She looked to be in her mid-to-late thirties, bleach-blonde hair that was teased well beyond health. She wore tight jeans, a low-cut bustier that only emphasized the fact that she couldn't fill out the bust, and her makeup was ridiculously heavy, the line of her foundation along her chin darker than the skin of her neck.

"What the fuck do you want, Jenny?" Alex demanded.

"I told you on the phone. I want to see my baby."

"She's not your fuckin' anythin', woman. Get that through your fuckin' skull."

"I have rights," Jenny yelled.

"You gave up those rights when you abandoned her," Alex ground out.

Jenny looked my way and raised an eyebrow. "This your new whore?"

Alex's hand reached for her throat so quickly, I couldn't help but gasp and stare at the floor.

"You fuckin' call her a whore one more time, or you fuckin' look at her one more time, I will end you," he threatened.

I looked up only when Jenny screamed and grasped her neck. Booker was between the two of them, his hand on Alex's shoulder. I forced back tears, my fear palpable as I watched the man I'd fallen in love with transform into someone I didn't recognize.

"Does she know how you like to fuck, Hawk?" Jenny continued to bait him. "Does she know how fuckin' warped you are? How you like to chain women up and hit them when you fuck them?"

The memory of the handcuffs flooded my mind and I swallowed down the bile threatening to spill. Alex glanced at me and his face hardened, but his eyes raged, and I had to look away.

"Out!" he snapped and my eyes met his again.

"What?" I rasped.

"Kayla, get her the fuck out."

"Me? Why?"

"Fuck off, Payton," he said, and scowled.

"But, Alex—"

"If I have to tell you again, babe, it'll be the last fuckin' time."

I felt wetness on my face and realized the tears I'd managed to hold back were now falling freely. I studied him through the haze of tears and his face remained emotionless, so I squared my shoulders, turned on my heel, and walked out of the room, as slowly and confidently as my shattered heart would allow.

NINE

Payton

IT DAWNED ON me relatively quickly that Dani was guiding my steps as we left the room. She led me through the foyer and out a side door, which opened onto an empty paved area with picnic tables and not much else. As soon as the cold hit me, I bent at the waist and vomited until there was nothing left in my stomach.

"Come sit down, honey," Dani said once I was calmer, and walked me to one of the picnic tables.

I lowered myself onto the bench and dropped my face into my hands, unable to stop the sobs that wracked my body.

"Payton, I'm so sorry," Dani whispered.

"I need to go," I said with a hiccup. "I have to get out of here."

"I know, honey." She nodded. "Kayla's getting the car."

"All my things are in Alex's saddle bags."

"We'll get them and either bring them to you or give them to Macey."

"Okay. Yeah, that'll work. Thanks."

Dani checked her phone. "Kayla's waiting out back."

"Do I…do I have to go back in there?"

"No."

"Okay, thanks."

I stood on shaky legs and followed Dani through a metal gate and into the parking lot at the back of the building. Kayla was waiting in the car, but stepped out when she saw me. "I have Lily buckled in and she's pretty much out for the count, so I'll drive you home."

I nodded and climbed into the passenger seat. Kayla and Dani talked for a minute and then Kayla slid back into the car and buckled up. We didn't speak as we headed out of the parking lot and away from the club.

I took several deep breaths as I stared out the window, trying not to completely break down…again.

"He'll calm down," Kayla said.

"It doesn't matter," I said, turning to look at her. "You heard him. He wants nothing to do with me."

"He loves you, Payton."

"You don't treat someone you love like that, Kayla."

"He's got some issues."

"Ya think?" I snapped, albeit quietly. "I saw the handcuffs, Kayla, and I don't think I could deal with that kind of sex, even if he claimed to love me."

"It's not a claim, Payton. He *does* love you."

"He choked her, Kayla." I blinked back tears again. "Wrapped his hand around her throat."

"What? No he didn't."

"Kayla, I saw it."

She pulled to a stop at a light and stared at me. "You can't have, because it didn't happen. He reached for her, but she backed away and Booker stepped between them."

"She was holding her throat and gasping for breath."

"Yeah, because she's a fuckin' drama queen, but Hawk did not choke her."

"It looked like he would have if Booker hadn't stepped

in."

She shook her head and pulled forward when the light turned green. "You don't understand everything."

"I don't think I *want* to understand everything," I returned.

"Shit," Kayla whispered, and glanced in the rearview mirror before focusing back on the road. "I'm going to tell you something that I've never told anyone else…and I'm pretty sure Hawk hasn't either."

"Don't betray his confidence, Kayla. Not to me. I can't imagine he'd like an ex to know something no one else knows."

"You're not an ex."

"Looks like you missed the memo, hon," I grumbled. "When a man tells you to fuck off, you're an ex."

"Put aside the fact that my brother's a moron for a minute."

I rolled my eyes, but didn't comment.

"Have you noticed that he doesn't drink anything he hasn't either opened or poured himself? If he sets it down, he doesn't go back to it?"

I shrugged. "I have noticed that, yes, but it never seemed weird to me. People often set drinks down at a party and forget about them."

"He doesn't forget," she said. "He does it because the bitch drugged him."

"I'm sorry?"

"Jenny. She drugged his beer."

"When?"

"About four years ago."

I gasped and glanced behind me. Lily was still asleep.

Kayla scowled. "She tied him to the fuckin' bed, drugged him and fucked him ungloved. Multiple times."

I felt sick again. "Are you saying she raped Alex in order to get pregnant?" I whispered.

"If you *ever* use the word rape, my brother will absolutely blow his fuckin' load. 'Men don't get raped.' Got it, Payton? If he finds out I'm telling you this, he'll kill me."

I nodded.

"And I say that figuratively. Hawk has never laid a hand on me in anger, or any woman for that matter…even Jenny."

I nodded again. I wasn't in the mood to argue with her, even if I wasn't entirely sure I believed her.

"I'm not sayin' I know anything about my brother's sex life, but I do know he'd never do anything anyone didn't want him to do," Kayla continued.

"I thought that too, until about twenty minutes ago."

"Please don't judge him too harshly."

"Kayla, I don't judge him at all. I love your brother. I'm hurt and a little frightened, but that doesn't mean I love him any less. Whether or not we'll be able to move past this? I just don't know if we can."

"I get it. Just believe me when I say he loves you enough to scare the shit out of him, okay? He knows you hate drama and Jenny's all drama." She glanced in the rearview again. "He thinks she'll drive you away from him."

"So, he's doing it before she can? I get it on a psychological level, but I thought he knew me better than that. I also thought he loved me more than that."

"He does, Payton. We've just kind of had a fucked up existence and he's trying to navigate the beauty of you in a sea of fucked-up-ness."

I nodded.

"As much as my brother and I are in sync and have each other's backs, we're really different," she continued. "When my dad went to prison, I was still a minor, so the court ordered counseling to help me deal with some of the shit my parents put me through. And it was the best thing that happened to me, honestly. But Hawk was an adult and there was no way in hell he was gonna go talk to anyone about what he went through, so I got some skills under my belt to deal. Him…not so much. When me and my ex were coming to an end, I decided to go back to counseling and it's what's kept me sane."

"That's good, Kayla."

"Please just give him a little time," she begged. "He'll come around."

"I can't promise that," I admitted.

"Will you try?"

I sighed. "I'll think about it."

She smiled. "That's all I ask."

"Do you mind dropping me somewhere else?" I asked. I wasn't quite ready to go home.

"No problem."

I let my mind drift as we headed to my brother's house, grateful Kayla left me to my thoughts. More of Alex came into focus for me now, and several questions I didn't think to ask were answered, but I still didn't know if it made a difference. Dating a man to "change" him was a losing battle and it just wasn't me.

Before I could dwell further on my maudlin thoughts, Kayla pulled up to the house and I gave her a sad smile. "Thanks for everything."

She squeezed my hand. "Don't give up on him."

"He has to not give up first, Kayla. Sucks to say that, but I'm not a woman who's interested in "fixing" a man."

She nodded. "God, I hope he pulls his head out of his ass."

"Me too, honey." I grabbed my purse and pushed open the door, stepping out and leaning down. "Drive safe." I glanced at Lily, still sound asleep, and my heart broke again. I bit back my sadness, closed the car door, and walked up my brother's driveway. Ringing the doorbell, I stepped from foot to foot as I waited for my brother to answer the door. I banged when he didn't answer right away, and wrapped my arms around me to ward off the cold…and the despair.

Brock pulled open the door, gun at the ready. "Pay?"

I burst into tears and slipped into his arms, wrapping my

arms around his waist. I heard the sound of Kayla's car drive off as he closed the door.

He rubbed my back. "Hey, what's all this?"

"I need to talk. But it has to be totally confidential."

"Always." Brock leaned back and frowned. "You know that."

I nodded and Brock followed me into the family room. I loved this room. Partly because I'd decorated it and even after Brock and Bailey had married and Bailey moved in, my sister-in-law loved it enough not to change it. Bailey was curled up on the sectional wrapped in a blanket, but she rose to her feet to hug me. "You okay?"

I shook my head.

Bailey smiled. "I'll make some tea."

"Scotch would be better."

"But you're mean on Scotch," Bailey said with a wicked grin.

I chuckled, my angry tears finally drying up. "Fine. Tea."

"Done," she said, and headed to the kitchen.

I lowered myself to the sofa, crossed my legs in front of me, and dragged my hands down my face. Brock sat next to me and faced me. "What's up?" he asked.

I licked my lips and studied him for a few seconds. "Hypothetically, say a man and a woman are having some kind of a weird and twisted sex-type relationship and she decides she wants this guy, but he has no interest in her other than sex…" I took a deep breath, and Brock frowned and cocked his head, but didn't comment. "So, one night she drugs him, ties him up, and has sex with him, which produces a baby."

"Hypothetically, that's fucked up," Brock said. "Not to mention, rape."

I nodded. "And then, hypothetically, say, the guy refuses to have sex with her ever again and she gives birth to a baby, dumping said hypothetical baby on his doorstep and disappearing for years. Only to show up now wanting the baby back."

"Fuck me, seriously? She did that to Lily?"

I sighed. "Well, yes…hypothetically."

Bailey handed me my tea and sat back where she'd been before.

I filled them in on the events of the night, leaving out Alex's more violent outburst and our private time in his room, and told them what Kayla had told me before dropping my head to my bent knees and groaning. "I'm not *so* naïve to think rape doesn't happen to men, but I mean, how many people do you come across who've dealt with it? I never have."

Brock frowned. "It happens more than you might think, but men aren't ones to freely admit it, so it's not reported as often as it should be." He squeezed my hand. "Rape doesn't always mean you're physically harmed, although, that's certainly the most common."

"I just don't know where to go from here. How do you process being dumped and all this crap happening on the same night?"

"You broke up?" Bailey asked.

"Most definitely. I'm not in the habit of staying in relationships with men who tell me to fuck off."

Brock sneered. "He told you to fuck off?" he ground out.

"Hypothetically," I rushed to say, realizing my folly of revealing that to my older, *very* protective brother.

"I will jack him up if he ever talks to you that way."

"I know, Brocky. But never fear, I can take care of myself." I stifled a yawn and smiled. "Sorry. I hate crying."

Bailey nodded. "It's exhausting."

"Very," I admitted.

"Do you want to stay?" Bailey asked.

"If that's okay," I said. "I don't have my car, so I'll hoof it home tomorrow."

Brock's home was only a few blocks from my parents', so it was a pretty easy walk.

"Come on," Bailey said, and rose to her feet. "You can

borrow my makeup remover and I'll give you something to sleep in."

"Thanks." I stood and my brother did the same, pulling me into a bear hug.

"You know you can tell me more," he said.

"I know," I whispered.

He kissed the top of my head. "Love you, sissy."

"Love you too."

I followed Bailey upstairs and into the guestroom where she left me to do my thing, which was to fall into bed and cry myself to sleep.

TEN

Payton

T HE BUZZING OF my phone on the nightstand woke me and I grabbed it, answering it without opening my eyes. "Hello?"

"Where do you want me to drop your shit?"

"Alex?"

"Where do you want your shit?" he repeated.

"What time is it?"

"Can you just fuckin' answer the question, Payton?" he snapped.

I sighed. "Are you drunk?"

"Fuck me, woman. I have your shit, I don't want it. Where the fuck do you want me to take it?"

The hurt came flooding back and I bit back tears. "Just give it to Dani. I'll get it from her."

"Are you fuckin' cryin'?"

I shook my head, but didn't answer him. Clearly, it was

over and he wanted nothing to do with me.

"Payton?" he snapped again.

I took a deep breath. "Just give the stuff to Dani, Alex. Thanks."

I hung up and shoved my face into the pillow, dissolving into tears. I felt sick and sad, hurt and angry, all at the same time. I'd never felt like this before, and quite frankly, being dumped by someone you loved totally sucked. I suddenly had a great deal of empathy for my exes.

My phone buzzed again and this time I checked the ID. "Hey, Dani."

"Hi. Sorry to call so late. I honestly thought I'd get your voicemail."

"It's okay. Alex woke me."

She let out a quiet hum. "I'm sorry honey."

"It's okay. He wanted to know what to do with my stuff, so I figured you two hadn't talked."

"Well, that's not entirely accurate."

I frowned. "I don't understand."

"He won't give me your bag."

"Can Kayla get it?"

"No." She groaned. "I debated on whether or not to call you, but he's locked himself in his room with a bottle of whisky and he's threatening to burn your things if we try to take them from him."

"Sounds like he's drunk."

"That's an understatement," she said. "What do you want me to do?"

"Honestly, there's nothing in there I can't replace. Just leave it. If he burns it, he burns it. It would be an apt ending to our relationship that went down in flames," I added somewhat pathetically. The call-waiting beep on my phone sounded and I glanced at my screen. "Ohmigod, he's calling again."

"Do you want to get it?" Dani asked.

"No. I'm just going to ignore him." I saw the time, just

after midnight. "I'm assuming Kayla's with Lily?"

"Yeah. I talked to her and they're fine. We're staying here tonight so Austin can keep an eye on Hawk."

"Okay. Sounds good." I rubbed my forehead, trying to stave off a headache. "Thanks Dani. Sorry to drag you into this mess."

"Don't worry about it. I'll still try to get your stuff."

"I appreciate that."

"Okay, better go," Dani said. "Talk to you tomorrow."

"Okay."

We hung up and I rolled onto my side and squeezed my eyes shut. My phone buzzed again, but it was Alex, so I ignored it. He continued to call well past midnight, so I turned off my phone and forced myself to sleep. Needless to say, I didn't really get any.

* * *

Sunday I awoke to the headache from hell…and a note from Bailey sitting on the kitchen counter.

Brock and I are at the store. Help yourself to coffee. Stay if you want, we'll be home in a couple of hours, but if you decide to head home, just lock up behind you. Love you!

I poured myself a cup of coffee and powered up my phone. Forty-two missed calls from Alex. I groaned. *Stalk much?*

No voicemails from him, which disappointed me. Again. Insane.

I rummaged in the fridge for breakfast, finding cream cheese and a ripe tomato, so I checked the pantry and found bagels. I loved my sister-in-law. She always bought the best food.

I was lifting the pastry to my mouth when the doorbell rang. I walked silently to the door and peeked out the side window, frowning to find no one there, but when I turned my eyes down, I saw my bag sitting on the porch.

I unlocked and opened the door, dragging my bag inside before glancing out to the street. Alex stood beside his truck looking as wrecked as me, his hair a mess, his clothes disheveled, and all I could think was how much I loved him.

He hesitated for a few seconds before walking toward me and I couldn't decide whether I should close the door on him or not. He stopped within hearing distance and grimaced. "Hey."

"Hi, Alex. Thanks for bringing my bag back."

"You're welcome."

"How did you know where I was?"

He slipped his hands into his pockets. "Your brother told me. Kayla said she dropped you off here."

Well, this was interesting information.

"You could have given my stuff to Dani," I whispered.

"Fuck, Payton, I'm sorry."

My composure crumbled and I burst into tears. I found myself wrapped in his arms and that just made things worse.

"Shh, baby, I'm so sorry," he whispered.

"I don't even know what you're doing here." I sniffed, but didn't pull away. "You told me to fuck off. Why didn't you just give the bag to Dani?"

"Because I love you." His fingers slid into my hair and tilted my head back. "I am a total fuckin' dick, baby, but I love you and I don't know how to apologize so this is alright again." He wiped the tears from my cheeks. "Tell me what to do. Anything, baby. I'll do anything."

"You scared me last night."

"I know, Payton. I'm so sorry." He sighed. "I know it's lip service right now, but I would never raise a hand to you. Please give me the chance to prove it."

"I don't want to be chained up and hit during sex, Alex."

"And you won't be. Kayla confessed she told you what happened with Jenny." A second of irritation crossed his face but he shook his head. "There's more to it that even she doesn't know. But, I will tell you everything…and I mean everything…and I promise, if you give me another chance once I do, you can make all the rules. Anything, baby. I mean it. Just tell me what I have to do."

I couldn't fathom what more there could be, but I knew he was telling the truth, and if he was willing to let me in so that I could make an informed decision, then I felt I should give him the chance. The fact I loved him played a little into that as well. I couldn't just turn off that emotion, but I also wasn't going to move forward blindly.

"Come in," I said, and pulled away from him.

"Are you sure you feel comfortable? Because we can wait until your brother gets back, or you can follow me somewhere public."

"I feel comfortable, Alex," I said. "I'll fill my brother in on what's going on and we'll go from there."

He nodded and followed me inside. I texted my brother, poured a cup of coffee for Alex and, after he said he didn't want breakfast, grabbed my bagel and sat with him on the sectional in the family room.

"Kayla filled you in on the stuff with Jenny, right?" he said.

I nodded as I chewed.

"Do you have any questions about it?"

"I don't think so. It's jacked up and I'd like to claw Jenny's eyes out, but no, I don't have any questions."

He seemed relieved and I figured he was probably pretty over the subject.

"My dad turned me onto porn when I was around ten. At the time, I thought it was twisted, but when puberty hit and all that that entails, things changed and I found myself obsessed with it I guess. I found girls fucked up enough to manipulate and I went with it. I lost my virginity at twelve, and I fuckin' loved sex…but when the girls didn't want to try the kinkier stuff, I realized that I either had to force them, which I would never do, just to be clear, or I had to go down a darker road when it came to sexual partners."

I sipped my coffee, trying to keep it down. I couldn't imagine a life where going down a 'darker road' was even an option, let alone a need.

"There were a couple of older high school girls that were up for anything and so I went wherever they'd let me go. Light bondage, spanking, stuff I don't need to go into detail about, but you can imagine. I remember saying something to my dad about it and he told me, fuckin' *told* me Payton, to do whatever the hell I wanted because they were askin' for it, and ultimately, they'd like it. That was the beginning of the end for me with him."

I nodded and continued to sip my coffee, not trusting myself to speak.

"And then he started eyeing Kayla."

I gasped. "Did he…?"

"She says no and I believe her because the second I recognized it, she was never alone with him. I'd sleep on her bedroom floor in front of her door the nights he'd get drunk. The only good drunk nights were when he'd pass out, but by the time I was fifteen, I could beat the shit out of him, so he knew not to mess with me."

"I'm sorry, Alex. That must have been hard."

He nodded. "Then I found the club. Or I should say, the club found me, and I discovered a safe place to land, so to speak. But it also opened a door to women willing to do anything that both excited and disgusted me. This brings us to Jenny. I slept with her once…and talk about warped. She's totally fucked up, baby, and coming from me, that's sayin' something."

"I picked up on that."

"I didn't want to touch her again, so, as you know now, she took matters into her own hands." He took a deep breath. "After she did what she did, I don't take any chances anymore. It's all within my control, but I never do anything someone doesn't want to do, so call it warped, called it depraved, but it's always consensual."

"But I can't do that," I whispered.

"I know, baby. I don't expect you to."

"I don't understand."

"Last night I realized that I trusted you. With everything. Well, until Jenny showed up, then I had a moment of doubt. But I didn't once feel the need to control anything with you. I was able to just let go and love you." He stroked my cheek. "I have never trusted anyone outside of Kayla, Payton. Until you. Even if you never wanted to see me again, I know you'd never breathe a word of this to anyone, and that's a lot to take in for me."

Ohmigod. I swallowed and took a deep breath.

"I know I scared you when I reached for Jenny and I won't try to excuse it, because there isn't one…I snapped I guess. But just know I have never done that before and I sure as hell won't ever do it again."

"Did you choke her?"

"What the fuck?" he snapped. "No!"

"Then why was she holding her neck and gasping for breath?"

"To fuck with you! I thought you got that last night."

"That's what Kayla said," I whispered.

"Baby, ask Dani. Ask Booker. I swear to God, I didn't hurt her, even though I wanted to." He grimaced. "I'm sorry I scared you."

I nodded. "Why did you tell me to fuck off?"

"Because you were scared, baby, and I'm a dick. I was angry that Jenny made me mad enough to want to kill her, and then when I saw your face, it was too much. I needed you gone. I'm not always good at the emotional shit, Payton, but I'll try. If you'll let me."

"Why didn't you give my stuff to Dani?"

"Because I had to see you," he admitted. "I knew if I let her have it, I wouldn't have an excuse to."

Well, that was kind of sweet.

"I know this is a lot to take in," he said. "If you need a couple of days, take 'em. I'll do whatever you want me to do. We can start slow again or you can tell me to fuck off. I'll respect your decision."

I nodded. "I should take some time to think."

"Whatever you need, baby."

"Would you mind dropping me home? I'd rather not walk."

"Of course."

I did our dishes quickly, left a note for Brock and Bailey, and then locked up and followed him to his truck. He threw my bag in the back and opened the door for me. We drove the five minutes to my parents' house and he parked in front.

"I need to be clear on something," I said before I climbed out of the truck.

"Okay."

I squeezed his arm. "Even if this doesn't work out for whatever reason, I need you to know my decision would have nothing to do with what you told me. I don't see you as anything less because of your past, or see you as warped or depraved…your words. I just need to figure out if we're right for each other."

He nodded. "I love you, Payton, and I'm not always gonna do everything right, but I do intend to fight for you. I'm not gonna lie about my intentions."

My stomach flipped. "I love you too, Alex. I'm just not sure if it's enough."

"I know, baby." He sighed. "I'll get your bag."

He helped me from the truck, handed me my bag, and then gave me the sweetest kiss he'd ever given me. I forced back tears as I navigated the sea of emotions.

"I love you," he said, and kissed my forehead before climbing in his truck and driving away.

I let myself into the house and walked down to my room, falling on the bed and bursting into tears for the forty-millionth time in less than a day.

* * *

Hawk

I stormed into the club, my mind solely on my directive. I'd come here the second I'd left Payton, my intention to take care of the threat immediately.

"Hey, Hawk," Train, one of the recruits, greeted.

"Hey, brother. Crow in his office?"

"Yeah, man."

I headed to the President's office, knocked on the door, and entered when bid.

Crow gave me a chin lift. "Hawk."

"No more Jenny," I demanded.

"Yeah, we're on it."

I wanted to say more… something in the vein of Crow making sure his old lady, Susie, was on board with the plan… but I held my tongue. I might be high up in the hierarchy of the club, but that didn't mean I could disrespect the Prez and his family.

"Everyone's on the same page, Hawk." Crow waved toward a chair. "Mack workin' on the legal shit?"

I nodded and sat down. "Bitch signed away her rights three years ago. That's not the issue."

"You got recruits on her, she can't get far."

"She's fuckin' wacked, Crow. I don't know what she'll do or who's still loyal to her."

"Mack helpin'?"

I nodded. "He's usin' his God-given gift to find out."

Logan 'Mack' Reed was the club's legal counsel. He happened to be Booker's closest friend and right-hand man, but he was also a damn good lawyer and I'd used him to deal with the Jenny situation in the beginning. Mack had had the foresight to get her to sign over her rights, something I wouldn't have thought of, and it meant Jenny didn't have a legal chance in hell of getting Lily back.

But she was devious and smart, so it didn't mean I

wasn't worried. Lucky for me, Mack was far more cunning and could work the system within the law. He was also charming, which meant he had his choice of women. All of whom he was 'working' to find out who still had ties to Jenny. I couldn't have been more grateful.

"Come in," Crow called when a knock at the door came.

"Hawk, honey, I'm sorry. I didn't know." Susie pushed in and sat in the chair next to me. "I mean, I didn't know she wasn't supposed to be there," she rushed on. "Not that she wasn't a psycho bitch."

I nodded.

"She said that Alana invited her, and I didn't know she was messin' with you. Both bitches are banned, honey."

"'Preciate that, Suz."

"You talk to Payton yet?"

I shifted in my seat. "Yeah."

Susie sighed. "I'm real sorry, Hawk. If I can make it right, you let me know."

I forced my heartache aside and nodded.

"Babe," Crow said. "We got business."

"Right," she said, and rose to her feet.

She started to leave, but Crow frowned. "Where the fuck are you goin', woman?"

She rolled her eyes and made her way to him, leaning down to kiss him quickly. "Fuckin' mixed messages, old man."

He smacked her ass and she chuckled as she left the office.

"You gotta miss church this week to deal with your woman, I'm good," Crow said.

I nodded, my appreciation unspoken as I stamped down the feeling of hopelessness.

"You get clear of this shit and I got a job for you."

I cocked my head. "Yeah?"

"Ashley's been gettin' threats. Bad break-up with some Russian fuckhead."

"You don't know him?"

"Nah and he's gone to ground. Darlin' daughter kept him secret. She won't do it again," Crow said, his voice low and angry. "Booker's lookin' into it, but when he finds the bastard, I'm gonna need you."

I nodded. "Anything yet?"

"So far, no, but we got a couple leads."

"Whatever you need."

"I'll keep you posted," Crow said. "If we see you at church, good, if we don't, good."

"Thanks, man," I said, and rose to my feet.

With a chin lift, I left my president's office and then headed out for the night.

# ELEVEN

Payton

MONDAY I SUFFERED through work. Luckily, my students were older which meant they tended to work quietly when instructed, but I was still exhausted and sad, and I missed Alex. Like my heart broke a thousand times in one day at the thought of not being with him.

At the end of the day, I headed home, surprised to find my mom in the kitchen. "Hi," I said. "You're home early."

She smiled. "I quit."

"What? You did?"

She nodded. "Took early retirement."

"Can you do that?"

"Apparently so. Your dad and I ran the numbers and it worked, so I quit. I gave them three weeks, but I need to burn up some vacation time or I'll lose it, so I'm only working one day at the end of that three-week period, and I'll still have five weeks paid vacation to cash out."

"Wow, Mom, that's awesome."

She studied me and then smiled. "What's up with you, honey? You look sad. How's Alex?"

I forced back tears again and made my way to the fridge, grabbing the O.J. from the top shelf. "It's been a rough couple of days."

"Want to talk about it?"

I poured a glass of juice and leaned against the island. "I don't know what to say. So much of it's complicated and I'm trying to work out if it's worth it."

"Honey, it's always worth it."

"What do you mean?"

"Let's sit," she said, and led me to the dinette table. I sat across from her and she squeezed my hand. "You've always been my careful one. You weigh the pros and the cons, make a graph and a chart, and then make your very informed decision based on the data you gather."

Does everyone think I'm a control freak?

"That being said, I don't worry about you…at least, not in the same ways I worry about your siblings. But that doesn't mean I don't worry about you in other ways. Alex is different than anyone you've ever dated and that boy loves you better than any of the others have." She smiled a little sadly. "He knows my baby. Truly knows her and that's more than any mother can hope for because I know he'll take care of you in all the ways that count."

"But you don't understand everything."

"I know, honey. And that part's where being an adult sucks, because it's ultimately your decision. Whatever way you go, you know Daddy and I will support you, and you know all of us will be here to help put your heart back together, but just know that we all love Alex, Kayla, and especially little Lily. They fit perfectly into our family."

"I know." I nodded, blinking back tears. "I really love him, Mom."

"But he scares you."

"So much."

"So did your dad, honey. He turned my world upside down in a way that rocked me to my core." She smiled again. "You and I are very much alike, Payton, so I'll give you a promise. When you take a risk, you reap really amazing rewards, and you will feel more alive than you ever have. It's worth it, honey, and I think *he's* worth it."

I sighed.

The house phone rang and my mom rose to her feet. "Hold that thought. Hello? Hi, Gordon." Her face fell and I sat up straighter. "Where is she? Yes. I'm coming now. We'll call everyone. Okay, honey. See you soon." She hung up and grabbed her keys. "Kris has been admitted. She's bleeding. They can't find the baby's heartbeat."

"Where is she?"

"Legacy."

I shot out of my seat, set my glass in the sink, and went for our coats. I fired off a group text to the rest of the family, knowing Mom would want to tell Dad herself, and then followed her into the garage.

As I climbed into my mom's car, all I could think about was I needed to talk to Alex. I was worried about my sister and I needed him to hold me and tell me it was all going to be okay.

Since I didn't know if I could talk without crying, I fired off a text to Kayla, filling her in on what was going on. Kayla and Kristen were getting close and I knew that if Kayla felt Alex should know, she'd tell him.

When we arrived at the hospital, Mom took advantage of the valet parking, and we rushed inside and up to maternity. Gordon was pacing the waiting room and Elizabeth sat crying on one of the seats, but she rushed to Mom and wrapped her arms around her waist.

My mom stroked her hair. "Hey, honey. It's okay."

I went to Gordon and gave him a quick hug. "Do you

need me to do anything at the office?"

Gordon and Kristen owned a pretty successful real estate company, and I had worked in the office during summer and school holidays during high school. It had been a great way to earn some money and get some administrative skills under my belt.

"No. I have an open house this weekend, but Sam's going to cover if I need him too. The paperwork's covered, so I'm set. But thank you."

"Well, if anything changes, let me know." I smiled. "Have you seen Kristen?"

He shook his head. "They're running tests. They won't let me see her until they're done."

"Okay," I said. I mean, what could I say? The whole thing was just awful.

We'd been at the hospital just over an hour when Gordon was finally called back to see Kristen. Elizabeth stayed with us, and by now, my dad, Anna, and Brock had arrived. Anna's husband, William was still at work so Bailey had offered to watch all the kids at my parents' house until we could get things figured out. Elizabeth wanted to stay with her parents, so she stuck close to my mom.

I was sitting with my face in my hands when Brock said, "Payton?"

"Hmm?" I looked up and he nodded toward the open hallway. I followed his nod and my heart raced. Alex was walking towards us and in that moment, I knew. I just knew he was it for me. No more guessing, no more worry. Just love.

I rose to my feet and rushed to him. He held his arms out to me and I slid into his embrace, squeezing my eyes shut as his hands moved to my hair. "I came as soon as I could, baby. Sorry it took a little while."

I bit back a sob and nodded.

"Any news?" he asked. I shook my head, and he stroked my back and pulled me closer. "Okay, honey. I've got you."

I don't know how long we stood there, but if anyone had asked us to move, I probably would have kicked them. It was Alex who broke the moment, suggesting we join the family, and leading me back to the waiting area.

My mom hugged him, as did Anna, and the men shook hands, and then he was all about me again, and I gladly accepted the support. We sat on a love seat type thingy and he had his arm around me while my back was to his side. As we waited for news, no one spoke, which was weird for us, but I think we were all afraid to say anything wrong.

Gordon walked into the room, his face grim as he sat beside my mom. "It's not good."

"Hey, Elizabeth," Alex said. "Will you help me grab some snacks from the cafeteria?"

I wanted to kiss him.

"Um, sure," she said, but I could tell she didn't want to leave.

"I'll fill you in when you get back," Gordon promised.

"Okay, Daddy." She stood in front of him. "Is Mommy okay?"

"She will be, sweetie."

Gordon hugged her and then Alex guided her out of the waiting area. Gordon broke down and it took a few minutes for him to gain his composure enough to speak. "They want to induce. There's no heartbeat."

My mom wrapped an arm around his shoulders and gave him a squeeze. Brock and Dad held it together, but the rest of us couldn't stop the tears.

"What does Kris say?" Mom asked.

"She's refusing to let them do it. Wants to see a miracle," Gordon said.

We'd all been raised in a somewhat loose Catholic family, but Gordon was an evangelical Christian and he and Kris had a pretty strong faith.

"What do the doctors say?" Mom asked.

"We can wait a day, maybe two, but any later and she

might be in danger.”

“Oh, honey,” Mom crooned. “This is a tough decision, but we know you’ll make the right one and we’re here. Whatever you need.”

My mom was the best person ever. None of us would survive without her.

“She’s so stubborn,” Gordon said.

A hint of a smile crossed my dad’s face. “She gets that from her mother.”

Now, bear with me here, because something happened that had never happened before. At least, none of us had ever seen it, and it was the most inappropriate thing on earth, but it also managed to do something none of us could imagine.

My mother (the supportive, gorgeous, G.I.LF. who always said and did the right thing…you’re tracking with me right?). Well, my mother flipped my father the bird. In the middle of the hospital waiting room. Just raised her middle finger and scrunched up her mouth...all silent and totally non-graceful like.

“Mom!” Anna exclaimed before the rest of us dissolved into much needed giggles. “Ohmigod, Dad, I blame you,” Anna continued. “She was sweet before you got hold of her!”

“How would you know?” my dad countered. “She could have been a bad influence on me.”

“Highly doubtful,” Anna grumbled, grinning like a loon.

Alex and Elizabeth returned, their arms laden with food and drinks, and he raised an eyebrow in my direction as I helped distribute food.

Needless to say, the mood wasn’t quite so heavy, which was a relief. Gordon pulled Elizabeth aside and filled her, age appropriately, on what was happening with Kristen, and then took her back to see her mom.

Once Kristen was settled in her private room, we all had a chance for a visit, albeit a short one, before it was time for us to let her rest. Gordon would stay at the hospital for as long as he could, so Mom and Dad took Elizabeth home with them. I was tasked with packing a bag for Kristen and Elizabeth, which Mom would bring back to the hospital when she brought Gordon dinner, so Alex drove me to Kristen's home and I went about packing.

Chance, their six-year-old Llasa Aapso, met us at the door and I realized that no one had mentioned what to do with him. "Would you mind grabbing his food from the pantry, honey? His leash and stuff should be on the second shelf. We'll take him back to my parents' house and go from there."

Alex nodded and I gave him a quick outline of the house, before he headed downstairs and I continued to throw things into an overnight bag for Kris. I dropped one bag in the hallway and moved onto Elizabeth's room. When I turned to grab her makeup, I jumped. Alex was leaning against the doorframe watching me.

"I need to put a bell on you."

He smiled. "Kinky."

I rolled my eyes.

"I grabbed the bag in the hallway and the food for Chance. Everything's in the truck."

"Thanks, honey."

"You okay?"

I zipped up Elizabeth's bag and sighed. "Honestly? I don't know."

"How about we head to your parents, drop everything off, and then eat on the boat?"

I smiled and nodded. "Sounds perfect."

He reached for the bag, but I grabbed his arm. "I love you," I whispered. "In case there was any question in your mind. I love you."

Alex slipped his hand to my neck and covered my mouth with his. I did my best to relay my love in a kiss, but that proved to be difficult to stop, and had he not broken the kiss when he did, I'm pretty sure we would have made love on my niece's bedroom floor.

"I love you, too," he said.

"Good thing you stopped."

He nodded. "We'll pick this up later."

I met his eyes. "Please, honey. I really don't want to wait anymore."

"Fuck, baby," he rasped, and kissed me again. He broke the connection quicker this time and stroked my cheek. "The boat."

I grinned. "Awesome."

I insisted on doing a little light housework before we left…making beds, doing dishes, and wiping down the kitchen counters and such. I knew Kris wouldn't feel up to it, and Gordon did all the cooking in order to avoid the housework (his words).

Once I was finished, we loaded Chance into the truck and took off for home. My entire family was in attendance, par for the course when something big happened…or something small. Pretty much all the time, really. Anna and Bailey were prepping food, Mom was playing with the kids downstairs, and William, Brock, and my dad were out on the deck grilling (and probably drinking beer).

I grimaced up at Alex and shook my head. He stroked my cheek and kissed me quickly. "No boat."

"Sorry," I whispered.

"Don't be, baby." He kissed my forehead. "I told you. Whatever you need."

"Do you think Kayla would want to bring Lily up?"

"I can call her."

"Do you mind?" I asked. "I like the idea of the whole family being here."

The front door opened just as Alex pulled out his phone, and Macey and Dallas walked in. I rushed to my friend and pulled her in for a hug. "You're here!"

"Where else would I be?" she challenged. "I brought wine."

"This is why you're my favorite."

Alex ended his call, greeted Macey and Dallas, and then we moved enmasse into the family room. Kayla and Lily arrived an hour later, and we sat as a family and ate dinner before my parents headed to the hospital.

The rest of the evening was a much needed distraction, even if we were missing a few of the clan, they were with us in spirit. Kayla and Lily fit right into the fold as they had on Thanksgiving, but it was different somehow. It was permanent this time and we all felt it.

We put the kids to bed, I called in sick to work, knowing I wouldn't be able to function at school the next day, and then the adults congregated in the family room with drinks and snacks. My parents arrived home sometime around ten, and rushed to join us.

"The baby moved!" Mom exclaimed, clapping her hands. "The bleeding stopped and they found the heartbeat. She has been ordered on bed rest for the remainder of her pregnancy, but the doctors are hopefully optimistic. If all is still good on Wednesday, she'll be released."

The relief we all felt was expressed loudly as we celebrated the good news as a group. Macey and Dallas left a little before midnight, as did Brock and Bailey, but Anna and William chose to leave soon after the good news had been relayed.

"We should go," Alex said after we'd said goodnight to Macey and Dallas.

"I don't want you to."

He chuckled. "I know, baby, but Kayla's got work tomorrow and Lily has school."

"Do you have to work?"

He shook his head. "I cleared my schedule in case you needed me."

"I don't think I could love you any more right now."

Alex grinned. "How about I pick you up and we'll eat lunch on the boat? If it's not too cold, we can take her out."

I licked my lips. "Yes, please."

He smiled and kissed me. "I'll call you in the morning."

"Okay."

"Love you, baby."

"Love you too."

He gathered a still sleeping Lily into the truck, while Kayla took off in her car, and after one more kiss my way, he left me standing on my parents' porch wishing I was going with him.

TWELVE

Payton

ALEX WOKE ME at ten the next morning and I was far too happy to hear his voice to be mad at him for calling so early. "Hi honey."

"You got fifteen minutes, baby."

I sat up. "What? No! I need an hour."

"Well, you got fifteen minutes."

I groaned. "You're a butt."

He laughed. "Fourteen."

"I'm hanging up now."

I took the fastest shower in history, pulled my hair into a ponytail, and dressed in record time. Since I never knew what to expect, I threw a few things into a backpack in case we actually got to be alone for more than five minutes, and headed upstairs.

Mom was in the kitchen, pouring a cup of coffee and she smiled when she saw me. "Hi honey. You're up early."

"Alex is picking me up and we're going to lunch." I

132

grabbed a travel mug of coffee. "How's Kristen? Is she up for visitors?"

"She's doing better and better and she said she'd like everyone to come around dinner if that works. She's liking the uninterrupted sleep she's getting."

I chuckled. "I bet." The doorbell rang and I screwed on the lid of the coffee. "Dinner's good for me," I said. "So I'll see you then."

"Okay, honey, have fun."

I pulled open the front door and launched myself at Alex. He laughed as he caught me and leaned down to kiss me. "I take it you missed me."

"So, so much," I confirmed.

"How hungry are you?"

"Starved."

"Burgerville?"

"Hells, yes, please," I retorted.

"Hi Alex," my mom called.

"Hey, Melissa." He grinned and separated himself from me. "I'll just say hi and then we'll go."

I wrinkled my nose, but his politeness won out, and he spent a few minutes chatting with my mother before we were finally on our way. Food acquired, we made our way to the marina, and then we were on the boat, and I couldn't wait to eat and then get him naked.

"This is the helm," Alex explained, and unlocked another door that had stairs leading down. The helm had a nice white chair that sat in front of the steering wheel and it sat up high for the best visibility. He led me down the narrow stairs and flipped on lights as we went. I had to admit, I was somewhat floored.

"Wow," I whispered.

Alex grinned. "This is the salon, at that end is the master stateroom and bathroom, and this end is the galley, and beyond the galley is another bedroom. That's the room that's not finished yet."

I turned to the nicely appointed kitchen, kind of like the one that had been in the big RV my parents had rented one year for a trip down the west coast. Very compact, but had everything one would need. There was a dining table, then bigger than expected sofas with a flat screen television, and Alex showed me the bathroom that would work nicely for Lily or guests. The room he was still working on was quite big and would hold four bunk beds.

We walked back through the salon area and into the master, where Alex dropped my bag on the king-sized bed. There was another bathroom attached to the bedroom and it had a shower, sink, and toilet.

We headed back to the salon and I removed my boots before sitting on one of the sofas and opening my bag of food. "What time do you have to pick up Lily?"

Alex sat beside me and handed me a napkin. "Kayla's got her."

"Your sister needs to be sainted."

"No doubt."

"So I have you for a few hours?" I grinned and bit into my burger.

"Or all night if you want."

I widened my eyes. "Really?"

"Yeah."

"We're meeting at the hospital around six and I have to work tomorrow, but I can always drive in from here if we can make it work."

Alex grinned. "We'll make it work."

I was suddenly very, very glad I'd packed a change of clothes. I finished my lunch, gathered my trash, and rose from the sofa. "I'm gonna brush my teeth and then I want you naked." Alex choked on the soda he'd just sipped and I chuckled. "Too forward?"

"You do your thing, baby, and I'll meet you in there."

I made a run for the bathroom, took a minute to check my appearance, and then brushed my teeth. I stripped down to my light blue lace bra and panties, and then stepped into the bedroom.

Alex whistled wrapping his arms around me with a grin. "Gorgeous, baby."

"Back atya." He wore nothing but his jeans and he was delicious. I slid my hands to his pecs and smiled. "Trust me?"

"All the way, baby."

"I trust you too, Alex." I patted his chest. "I need you to hear me on that."

He nodded and kissed me, unclasping my bra and tugging it down my arms. I slid my hands into his hair as he lifted me and settled me on the bed, then stretched out beside me. He drew a nipple into his mouth and bit down gently. I arched into his mouth as he continued to shower attention on my breasts while sliding a hand under the waistband of my panties and between my legs.

His finger slid through the wetness and then slipped inside of me. I groaned and pushed against him as he slid another inside. His thumb found my clit and I moaned. I could feel my orgasm building, but before it washed over me, he removed his hand.

"Don't stop," I demanded as he stood. "Where are you going?"

He pushed his jeans from his hips and I grinned. God, he was magnificent. After he slid my panties from my hips, he slid on a condom and rose up above me, settling his hips between mine and guiding himself inside of me. I wrapped my legs around him and arched up.

"Fuck, baby." He slid out of me and then back in slowly. "God, you feel so good."

"More, Alex."

He covered my mouth with his and thrust deep inside of me.

"Yes," I whispered against his lips.

His tongue slid into my mouth as his cock surged deeper

and deeper, faster and faster. I broke the kiss and moaned. "Yes!" I called out.

I felt my orgasm build and relished the feeling, but when his hand slid between us and his finger found my clit, it was over and I exploded around him. I screamed out his name as I gripped his biceps and tried to catch my breath.

Within seconds, I felt Alex's cock pulsate inside of me and he kissed my neck as he rolled us onto our sides. "I'll make that last a little longer next time."

I couldn't help but chuckle. "I was doing fine until you added that little clit action at the end."

He grinned, kissing my chin. "God I love you, Payton."

"Love you too." I looped my arms around his neck and wove my fingers in his hair. "You're not bad at this sex thing, honey. I quite enjoyed that." He dropped his forehead to my chin and I felt his body shake with laughter. I kissed the top of his head and grinned. "I hope you have a *lot* of condoms."

His body stilled. "Yeah, baby. I have enough." He smiled and kissed me before sliding out of me and heading to the bathroom. "I got tested last week."

I leaned up on my forearms. "For?"

He returned and stood at the edge of the bed wrapping his hands around my thighs. "For everything. I should get the results by Friday. You on the pill?"

"Yes. Do you want me to get tested?"

"When's the last time you were with someone?"

"Two years ago."

"Were you clean two years ago?"

I wrinkled my nose. "Yes, honey, I am most definitely clean."

He pulled my body down the bed, causing me to fall onto my back again, and sliding my legs over his shoulders. "Then, no. You don't have to get tested."

I shifted as his mouth kissed his way down the inside of my left thigh. He gripped both of mine and found my eyes.

"Don't move. Get me?"

I took a deep breath and bit my lip, dropping my head back to the mattress. He lowered his mouth to my clit and sucked until I couldn't help myself from bucking my hips. He gripped my thighs tighter and lowered my bottom to the bed, spreading my knees. I whimpered as he sucked harder, slipping a finger inside of me. I slid my hand into his hair and arched against his mouth.

Without warning, he stood, pulling me further down the bed, and slammed into me. I cried out and arched again.

"Too much, baby?" he asked.

"God, no. Harder, Hawk."

He grasped my thighs again, holding them against his hips and lifting me slightly as he surged into me. I fisted my hands in the comforter, somewhat unable to do much else because Alex had me anchored to his body. He thrust into me again and again, his body locked as he held me to him. I cried out as I came around him, but didn't have time to enjoy it as I was flipped onto my stomach and taken from behind.

I steadied myself on all fours and Alex reached around me to cup my breasts. His movements were slower now, which only managed to drive me crazy. "You okay?"

I pressed back into him. "Yes."

He squeezed my leg gently. "Wider, baby."

I widened my legs immediately and his hand left my breast and found my clit. I groaned, grinding against him. He slid in slowly again and I sighed. "More, honey."

"Patience, baby."

I reached between us as he slid out of me again and wrapped my hand around his cock. "Screw patience, Hawk. I want you to fuck me."

He pushed into my hand and I released him. He hissed. "Fuck."

"Yeah," I retorted. "Gonna take care of me, handsome?"

Alex slammed into me again and I cried out in relief. His thrusts came harder until I exploded around him and my face hit the mattress, then he surged in two more times and I felt his cock pulse as he came inside of me. He kissed my lower back and then my bottom, before sliding out of me and heading to the bathroom to get rid of the condom.

I let my body fall to the mattress, my legs nothing but jelly, and smiled as he returned to the bed. "Well done, honey. I quite liked that as well."

He laughed and stretched out beside me, pulling me into his arms. "You're bossy in bed, baby. Didn't peg you that way."

"Liar."

He laughed again. "You got me."

I nuzzled his neck and sighed. "I can honestly say, not only have I never had an orgasm that intense, I was sure women who said they had multiples lied."

"I plan to give you a few more before this day is over, baby."

"Can't wait." We lay in silence for several minutes, the sound of the water lapping against the boat calming. "You know the stuff you did with other women?"

His body locked. "Babe, that's over."

I leaned up so I could look him in the eye. "Would you ever do that with me?"

Alex stared at me and frowned. "No."

"What if…what if I'd like to?"

"Fuck, baby. Are you serious right now?"

"I don't know if I want to be chained or whipped or whatever, but handcuffs might be fun, and I've kind of always wanted to find out what it felt like to be spanked."

Alex shook his head.

"I don't know if I'm into everything that might involve a red room of pain, but some of it sounds kind of sexy."

"Fuck me," he whispered, and then groaned.

"Just a thought."

He rolled me onto my back and kissed me before dropping his forehead to mine. "We can do whatever you want,

Payton. Anytime you want. You just let me know. And for the record, I have never chained or whipped anyone."

"Okay." I smiled, biting back a yawn. "Right now, I just want to sleep in your arms and listen to the sound of the water."

"You can listen to the sound of the water while you sleep? That's quite a trick."

"Bite me."

He chuckled, rolling over me slightly and smiling. "Later." He kissed me gently and then adjusted the covers around us, pulling me back onto his chest.

I smiled as sleep took me, safe and warm in his arms.

* * *

I came awake with a moan as a strong hand slid between my legs and cupped me gently before fingers slipped inside.

"Time to wake up," Alex whispered, and raised himself above me, settling his hips between my legs. "Spread, baby."

I spread for him and he slipped inside of me as I wrapped my legs around him. He anchored his arms to the bed and drew in a nipple as his hips jerked back and thrust in. He did this slowly until I cried out in frustration, and then he slammed in again and again until I came. With one more pull of my nipple, he came as well, and then slipped out of me and pulled me onto his chest.

I kissed his neck. "Well, that's a nice way to wake up."

"Anytime you want me to wake you like that, baby, just say the word."

I chuckled and snuggled closer. "The word."

Alex laughed.

"What time is it?"

"Five."

"Shit." I shot up and scrambled over him. "Honey, we have to go. If we're going to pick up Lily beforehand, we're going to be late. There'll be traffic."

He sat up slightly. "I didn't realize we were picking Lily up."

"We can't have a family dinner without her, Alex." I tapped my temple. "Think, honey." I stared incredulously at him as I pulled on my panties and he looked confused. "What?"

"I hadn't planned on staying. I was going to drop you off and pick you up when you were done."

I frowned. "Oh, okay. If that's what you want to do."

He climbed off the bed and I bit my lip to keep myself from sighing. Clothed he was gorgeous, naked he was illegal. "If you want me there, baby, you just have to say so."

I clasped my bra and rolled my eyes. "I already did."

"When?"

"*Hello*, when I told you we were having a family dinner!"

"Yes, *you're* having a family dinner, baby. With *your* family."

I hunted around for my socks, finding one inside my boot. The other was on the floor next to it. "*My* family *is* your family, Hawk, or do you not want them?"

"Payton." He raised his hands in surrender. "I'm not trying to start a fight, honey. I just didn't want to invite myself to something if you didn't want me there."

I stomped my foot. "Sometimes, Hawk, I want to hit you."

He dropped his head back and started laughing, so I *did* hit him. Gently…but it was in the stomach, so he wasn't expecting it.

"Fuck," he said, but still managed to continue laughing.

"Why are you laughing?" I demanded.

He wrapped his arms around my waist and pulled me to him. "Because you're standing in the middle of the bedroom on my boat, yelling at me while wearing nothing but your bra and panties…and one sock."

I huffed and raised the hand with the other sock in it. "Well, you interrupted me."

He leaned down and rubbed his nose against mine. "Fuckin' adorable, baby."

"Get dressed." I smiled and stepped away from him, dragging my sock on before finding the rest of my clothes. "And for the record, whenever there's a family *anything*, you, Lily, and Kayla are included in it, because you're stuck with us whether you want to be or not."

I yanked on my jeans and Alex pulled me to him again. "I want to be."

"Good answer."

He kissed me quickly and we finished dressing.

THIRTEEN

Payton

KAYLA OPTED OUT of dinner, seemingly relieved she had a night to herself. "I'm going to soak in a hot tub, drink a beer, and watch a movie my brother can't interrupt with some bullshit comment."

I chuckled. "You go girl."

She hugged me and grinned. "Thanks for the invite, though."

"It's an open one, Kayla. Seriously. Anytime."

"Will there be ice cweam?" Lily asked.

"I bet if there isn't any at the hospital, we can find ice cream somewhere else later," I said.

She let out a squeak and jumped up and down. "Wet's go!"

I chuckled. "How about you go potty first?"

Lily frowned but did as she was told. I helped her wash her hands and then we met Alex at the front door. He had our coats and helped us into them before heading out to the truck.

Alex and Kayla lived in Beaverton in a surprisingly sub-urban ranch on a quiet street. The house was small, just three bedrooms and one bathroom, but well kept, and although it was masculine inside, it didn't scream "biker" when you walked in. Alex bought it three years ago and mostly chose it for its proximity to decent schools for Lily's sake.

The bummer of it was, it was super far from me, so we were going to have to have a serious conversation about living arrangements for the future.

I smiled.

We had a future.

"What's got you grinnin', baby?" Alex asked, and linked his fingers with mine.

I turned my head still leaning against the headrest, and smiled again. "I'm just happy."

"Fuck," he whispered.

"What's wrong?"

"Nothin', just gotta figure out how to make you smile like that forever."

"Alex," I said on a sigh. "Love you."

He lifted my hand to his lips.

"Daddy?" Lily said.

"Yeah, baby girl."

"Can we wisten to Fwozen song? Pweeese."

"Ohmigod, you don't have the CD do you?" I whispered.

He grinned. "I don't have the song, baby girl. How about Guns 'n Roses?"

I looked back at her. She wrinkled her nose, but then just as quickly, smiled. "Nobemba Wain."

Alex chuckled. "Okay, baby girl."

He released my hand and chose *November Rain* from the *Use Your Illusion* CD and I chuckled. "Well played, honey…well played."

The song lasted until we crossed into Vancouver. Alex turned the stereo off and we arrived at the hospital just before six. "Record time, honey," I said.

He grinned. "And you were worried."

"You were just lucky we didn't hit much rush hour."

Alex chuckled and we unloaded Lily from the car and headed up to Kristen's room. I peeked into the room to make sure she still felt up to visitors, and found my entire family, plus Macey inside. "Alex and Lily are here," I said.

"The more the merrier," Kristen said brightly.

We joined the group and Lily rushed to Elizabeth and the other kids in the corner where someone had set a couple of pizzas. With her occupied, Alex and I hugged Kristen and then grabbed pizza and fell into comfortable conversation with the family as we ate.

This was our perfectly adequate little world for the next three weeks. And when I say perfectly adequate, I mean that we were in sync, we were in love, we were building a bond that no one could break…but it was also wrought with the stark reality that we led very different lives, and when it took an hour to get to one another's homes, we had very limited time together most days. Add in the fact that there was a little girl in the picture; sex was often a stolen few minutes whenever we could find it, and was usually over far too quickly.

The bottom line…I needed to get my own place.

The Friday before winter break, we had a rare night to spend together because Kayla offered to watch Lily for us. I was sprawled over a deliciously naked Alex in the middle of the stateroom bed on the boat, having just come four times, and I was trying to figure out a way to bring up the subject of the future without saying, 'hey, let's talk about our future.'

"Babe, spit it out," he said, and chuckled.

"Spit what out?"

He gave my bottom a gentle smack. "I can hear you thinking."

I sighed and settled my chin on top of my hands on his

chest. "I need to find a house."

"Yeah."

I shrugged with a smile. "That's it."

Alex laughed. "Baby, you're fuckin' adorable when you're lyin'."

I groaned and rolled onto my back.

He leaned over me and slid his hand to my neck. "Tell me."

"Okay, but stay with me here, because I'm going to verbally process for a bit."

"Break it down for me, Payton."

"You live in Oregon and I live in Washington."

"Good start, baby."

"Bite me," I retorted, and grinned when he nipped my neck. "Mmm, more of that later."

He sat up and chuckled. "Promise."

"So, I have a dilemma because I don't want to live in Oregon. Partly because their schools kind of suck…sorry, but they do…and I don't want to take a ten percent hit to my paycheck with taxes. Plus, I know this might be weird, but we all live close to each other and I don't know if I could live all the way in Beaverton…not that I'm saying I'm asking to move in with—"

"Baby, take a breath."

I wrinkled my nose, but did what he suggested.

"I'm not married to Beaverton, Payton," he said. "I bought that house because at the time it was close to the club and work, and I needed a tax write off."

My heart raced. "Oh."

"So, I agree, you need to find a place, but you want to stay in Washington, I can move to Washington."

"Seriously?" I asked. "You'd move for me?"

He frowned. "I'm thinkin' I'm fuckin' everything up now."

"What? Why?"

"'Cause you haven't figured out I'd do anything for

you."

I pushed him onto his back and straddled his hips. "You, Alex James, are about the most perfect man alive."

He grinned as he ran his hands up my thighs. "So when I ask you to marry me, you'll say yes?"

"I guess you'll have to ask me and find out," I retorted. "But I'm not into the whole living together before marriage thing, so our immediate issue is still the same."

"What's your problem with living together?"

"Outside of the fact that my parents would have a coronary, there's evidence that couples who live together before marriage divorce more than couples who don't. I learned it in one of my psych classes years ago." I leaned down and kissed his stomach, his muscles constricting at my touch. "And I plan to only marry once." I kissed him just above his lily tattoo. "Divorce isn't an option…but, hear me on this, honey…murder is."

He laughed and I grinned down at him. "So you'll go to jail for murder, but you won't divorce. Got it," he said.

"You're a smart cookie, honey." I shifted so I was between his knees. I kissed my way up and down the length of his hardening cock, sliding the tip into my mouth with a gentle suck.

"So the conversation's over?" he rasped.

"For now," I said, and took his length deeper into my mouth.

"Fuck," he whispered, and gripped my hair.

I wrapped my hand around him and moved up and down in sync with my mouth. Without warning, I lost purchase on his cock and found myself dragged under him. "Hey! I wasn't done."

He slid into me, covering my mouth with his as he reached between us and fingered my clit.

"Ohmigod," I breathed.

"So fuckin' wet," he whispered against my neck.

"Sucking you off tends to do that to me."

He buried himself deeper. "Someone's in a sassy mood."

I arched against him. "When I'm interrupted while sucking you off, it tends to put me in a sassy mood, handsome, so how about you take care of me so I can get back to what I was doing."

His eyes met mine. "Do you want to play, Payton?"

"That depends," I said.

"On?"

"On whether or not I get to finish."

He smiled. "I'll let you finish. But how far do you want me to go?"

"I don't know, Alex, I've never done anything like this before. Should we have like a safe word or something?"

"Stop works."

"Sounds a little boring," I grumbled.

Alex's smile deepened. "You pick."

I licked my lips, my body primed, and the fact that he was still buried inside of me didn't help me focus. "Porthole."

He dropped his head and his body shook as his laughing grew louder.

"I didn't know I was supposed to get creative," I cried. "It's the first thing I could think of."

"What's your least favorite color?" he asked, and raised his head.

"Um, I don't know…chartreuse?"

"Give me something shorter."

"Green."

"Okay." He slid out of me and off the bed. "Green's our safe word. If you use it, I'll stop. I'll also stop if you ask me to stop. But I'll still ask you before I do anything and if you don't want to do it, we won't do it."

"I trust you."

He smiled again. "I don't have much to play with, baby, but we'll improvise."

He left the room and I took a minute to pee.

When he returned, he had a belt and a length of rope. "Give me your hands," he instructed.

I held them in front of me and he tied them together, kissing each palm as he tightened the rope. "Too much?"

I shook my head.

"Stand here." He positioned me where he wanted me, facing away from the bed. "Spread your legs and raise your arms."

I did as he said and he threw the length of rope he'd left hanging between my tied arms over one of the rods on the ceiling. Alex explained they'd been put there as part of the previous owner's design and although Alex didn't follow the drop curtain décor, he left the rods. Now I was thinking his decision was brilliant.

"Spread more, baby."

I did, which lowered me closer to the floor.

"Okay?"

I smiled and nodded. This was so freakin' hot.

"Tug on your hands," he said.

I did. They didn't budge.

Alex ran his hands down my extended arms. "You still okay?"

I smiled. "So far."

He cupped my breasts, kissing each of them. "Beautiful, baby."

Sliding his hands down my sides, he knelt before me, kissing me intimately before sucking on my clit. I whimpered as he blew gently over the area he'd just licked and on autopilot reached for him, but my arms wouldn't budge. I felt the tingle between my legs and then he sucked again and I knew I was wet.

"Slide your legs over my shoulders," he instructed, and I did, which meant his face was right where he wanted it to be. "Perfect."

He gripped my bottom as I was suspended from the ceiling, and forced to use my legs to hold onto him, but it was when he covered my core with his mouth that I realized I was probably going to come far too quickly for my liking.

With his mouth he drove me into a frenzy, and when he slipped his finger inside of me, I cried out, but it was when his palm connected with my ass that I exploded around him.

I didn't have time to enjoy my post coital-type high, as he lowered my legs to the ground before picking me up again and driving into me from a standing position. He guided my legs around his hips and held my bottom to him as he thrust in. I yanked on my arms frustrated with the fact that I couldn't touch him, but God, it was hot. He drew a nipple into his mouth and slapped me again, which caused my pussy to contract which in turn threw me into another orgasm.

I dropped my head back and screamed. Alex's hands slid up my back, one holding me tight, the other releasing my hands. I wrapped them around his neck and he carried me to the bed, lowering me to the mattress and pulling my bottom to the edge. Still inside of me, he pushed my knees back and thrust into me. I took some of my power back and raised my legs, settling them against his chest. He grasped my thighs and continued to bury himself in me until he grunted and released my legs, falling on top of me and rolling me to face him.

"Holy fuck," he rasped.

I ran my hand over his jaw. "Um, yeah. That's a good description."

Alex ran his hands over my arms. "You feel okay?"

I laughed. "That was the hottest, most amazing thing on the planet honey. I came like a million times before you untied me." I kissed him quickly. "For the record, I apparently like to be spanked."

He grinned. "Yeah, I got that."

I sighed. "Does this make me warped?"

"Baby, we're both consenting adults in a committed relationship. No it doesn't make you warped. It makes you more than I could have ever hoped for."

"Same, honey. I don't think I could love you more if I tried."

"You got the next two weeks off, right?"

"I do."

"You gonna stay with me a couple of nights?"

I grinned. "Do you want me to stay?"

"I want you to stay the whole two weeks, but I know that won't happen."

I chuckled. "No, but only because Mom has a buttload of stuff for us to do before Christmas, but I can definitely stay for a few days."

"Lily's gonna lose her shit."

"What are we doing for her for Christmas? Do you want to do something at your place in the morning before my parents'?"

"She wakes up and Santa hasn't come, we'll have an issue, so yeah, probably do something at my place in the morning."

"Do you want me to stay Christmas Eve or is it too soon for that?"

Alex chuckled. "It's not too soon, baby. Lily's already asking daily if you're gonna be her new mommy."

"She is?"

"Yeah." He ran his hand over my bottom.

"And what do you tell her?"

He shook his head.

"You tell her no?"

"*No*." He gave my bottom a gentle smack. "What I tell her is not going to be repeated just yet. You'll know when the time is right."

I leaned over him and narrowed my eyes. "I have ways of making you talk, Mr. James."

"You do?"

"Yes…plus you promised I could finish what I started earlier."

He chuckled, linking his hands behind his head. "I'm all

yours, baby."

Needless to say, he didn't squeal, but I didn't care because I got to finish what I started.

FOURTEEN

Payton

CHRISTMAS EVE, ALEX insisted on picking me up from home and driving me to his house since we'd be back up this way the following afternoon. This was the excuse he gave me, although, he always insisted on driving regardless of the reason, so I wasn't buying it.

He spent a few minutes chatting with my parents while I made sure I wasn't missing anything and then we drove down to Beaverton to find a very excited Lily waiting at the door.

"Payton!" she squealed and launched herself at me, wrapping her arms around my neck as I lifted her.

"Hey, baby. Are you all ready for Santa?"

Her head bobbed up and down. "Unh, huh. Are we gonna bake cookies?"

"Of course we're going to bake cookies," I said as we walked into the living room. "I even bought carrots for the reindeer. *And* I brought a movie we could all watch together while we eat cookies. How does that sound?"

"I love you, Payton."

I chuckled and hugged her tighter. "Love you too, baby."

Kayla walked into the room and gave me a hug after I'd set Lily on her feet. "Welcome."

"Thank you."

"Are we baking cookies or what?" she asked.

"Cookies, cookies." Lily rushed for the kitchen and opened the fridge.

"Hold up, baby girl, let's get prepped first," Alex said.

I shrugged out of my coat, which Alex took from me, and then headed into the kitchen. After washing our hands we grabbed all the ingredients for chocolate chip cookies and, since Alex was on dinner duty, we let him relax while we baked.

I don't remember a time when I'd had more fun. Lily and I kept sneaking spoonfuls of cookie dough when Kayla wasn't "watching," and Lily thought it was the greatest thing ever. Kayla played along and we chuckled all the way through the four dozen cookies we managed to bake. I should probably note that we'd made enough for five dozen cookies, but it couldn't be helped, raw cookie dough is impossible to resist.

After dinner (Alex made a spaghetti bolognaise to *die* for) I helped Lily with her bath and getting ready for bed, before we piled onto the sofa, me between her and Alex, a blanket covering us and *Rudolph the Red Nosed Reindeer* cued up and ready to play.

Kayla handed me a glass of wine and then sat in the overstuffed chair by the fire.

It took forever to get Lily to actually fall asleep once the movie was done. I was required to read three stories before Alex shut it down and forced me out of the room.

"Daddy what if Santa doesn't come?"

"Santa's comin' baby girl. I promise." He smiled. "But

he's not comin' 'til you fall asleep. And believe me, he'll know."

She let out a frustrated groan, but lay down and closed her eyes tight. I forced myself not to laugh. She was trying so hard to be good, but she was fighting her desire to see Santa come down the chimney.

"Lily," Alex said.

"I'm asweep, Daddy, I can't hear you," she whispered.

I slapped my hand over my mouth and stepped further away from the door.

"I love you, baby girl," he whispered.

"Wuv you too, Daddy. I wuv you Payton," she said.

"I love you too, honey," I said, and Alex closed the door.

Alex wrapped an arm around me from behind and kissed the back of my neck. "You smell incredible. I have wanted to peel your clothes off your body for hours."

I chuckled. "It's the cookies."

"Wanna make out on the sofa?" he asked as he led me into the living room.

"What if Santa catches us?" I faced him, wrapping my arms around his neck. "We might be instantly relegated to the naughty list."

"He'll take one look at you and know I couldn't give a shit if I am."

"So romantic."

Alex smiled and kissed my forehead. "Thank you, Payton."

"For?"

"Making tonight perfect. I have never seen Lily so happy."

"Honey, you don't have to thank me. I love hanging out with her." I stroked the back of his neck. "You're an amazing daddy, Alex. I couldn't be more impressed with you."

His mouth covered mine and we spent a few minutes making out in front of the Christmas tree.

"Don't mind me," Kayla said, and broke the moment.

I chuckled. "Sorry."

"Don't be sorry, hon. You guys can kiss all you want, just so long as I don't see either of you naked, it's all good."

"Promise," I said. "I'm going to get drinks, then we have to watch *A Christmas Story*."

"What's that?" Kayla asked.

"You've never seen *A Christmas Story*?" I asked in horror. "It's like a tradition."

"We didn't have a lot of those, baby," Alex revealed.

"Well, then we're starting one tonight. Lily's a little too young, but we're not, so we're going to watch the magic of one of the best Christmas movies of all time."

"I'll get it cued up," Alex offered.

"I set it next to the TV, honey," I said, and headed into the kitchen.

When I returned, I handed beer to Alex, nog to Kayla, and set my wine on the side table before snuggling next to Alex.

"You could have opened it, baby," Alex whispered, and twisted off the beer cap.

I smiled. "Next time."

"Love you."

I wrapped my arm around his waist and kissed him quickly. "Love you too."

Alex and Kayla loved the movie, as I suspected, and Kayla headed off to bed shortly after it was done. Once Alex confirmed Lily was dead to the world, we snuck her present from Santa under the tree and headed to bed. After a very quiet but satisfying lovemaking session, I fell into a deep sleep sprawled across Alex.

* * *

"Santa came! Santa came!" a tiny little voice squealed and then the body attached to that voice jumped onto the bed.

"Shhh, baby girl," Alex grumbled. "Payton's still asleep."

"Payton," Lily whispered, and patted my face. "Santa

came.”

“That’s awesome, honey.” I forced my eyes open and wrapped my arm around her, pulling her between me and Alex. “How about you give me and daddy a minute to wake up and we’ll come see what Santa brought you.”

“Okay!” She jumped off the bed as quick as she’d come and rushed out the door.

I rolled back onto Alex and sighed. “What time is it?”

He grabbed his phone and then set it on the nightstand again. “Six.”

“Going forward, we have to have a rule…no waking Mommy and Daddy before nine.” Chalk it up to my exhaustion, but it took me a minute to realize what I’d said. “I mean—”

“Don’t, baby,” Alex interrupted. “Don’t you dare backtrack on that one.” He rolled me onto my back and smiled. “I love that. You have no idea how much I love that, but I love that.”

I smiled and nodded. “’K.”

“Come on. Let’s get coffee.”

We rolled out of bed and Alex pulled on a pair of pajama bottoms and a T-shirt. I had worn shorts and a T-shirt to bed, considering I was not in my own home and I didn’t feel comfortable enough to wear a cami and undies like I normally did.

We arrived in the living room to find Kayla sitting in the chair by the fire, staring blankly at the tree while sipping a cup of coffee.

“Merry Christmas,” I said brightly.

Kayla shook her head. “Gimme a minute.”

“Mewwy Kissmas,” Lily said, and rushed to sit in front of her stocking. “Can I open pwesents now?”

“We’re gonna get coffee and then we can open, baby girl,” Alex said.

We did our best to pour quickly, and then Alex finally let

Lily just go for it. I had to give it to her; she was a lot more patient than I typically am on Christmas morning.

"Santa" had brought Lily a Princess Elsa doll, Kayla bought her a microphone, and Alex and I together bought her a full Elsa dress up costume. To say that her head nearly exploded with excitement was an understatement. Once she'd calmed down a bit, we exchanged gifts with each other and Kayla and I ended in a puddle of giggles to find we'd bought each other the same gift, only she'd bought me the understated pair of hoop earrings and I bought her the huge ass, hang to her neck ones.

Alex loved the black leather cuff watch I bought him and I was blown away by the really pretty diamond bracelet he bought me. It would go perfectly with the red, wrap dress I planned to wear to dinner. All in all, this Christmas was shaping up to be perfect.

Lily really wanted to wear her Elsa costume to my parents', so we dressed her up, I did her hair, and then we packed a change of clothes for her and piled into the truck. Kayla was driving separately because she had plans with friends the next day and we didn't know how late we'd be.

We were the last to arrive, so the kids were extremely glad to see us (they were forced to wait for us before opening gifts). Dallas and Macey had apparently arrived ten minutes before us, so I hugged them, exceedingly glad Dallas had Christmas off.

"Now Daddy?" Lily whispered (loudly) once everyone was done with gifts.

He grinned and rose to his feet, leaving me on the sofa sitting next to Macey. "What's going on?"

Alex and Lily pow-wowed in the corner and then Lily came to me, her hands behind her back. "I have a qwestin," she said.

I glanced at Alex and then back at her. "Okay."

"I want to know if you'll be my mommy."

Alex knelt in front of me, pulled Lily onto his extended

knee, and then helped her open the ring box. "Will you marry us, Payton?"

I scanned the room and realized my entire family knew this was going to happen. My mom was sniffling, my dad looked like the cat that ate the canary, Macey was nearly sobbing, and everyone else just watched in delight.

I grinned back at Alex, forcing back my own tears. "I would be honored to marry you and be Lily's mommy."

Lily squealed and threw herself in my arms. "Can I caw you Mommy now?"

"Of course, you can, baby," I whispered, tears freely streaming down my face now.

"My turn, baby girl," Alex said, and pulled me to my feet once Lily had climbed off my lap. He slid the ring on my finger and pulled me into his arms, kissing me a little more chastely than normal, but it was still awesome.

I didn't even get a chance to study the ring before my family descended on us with congratulations and hugs. Just before dessert was served, Alex and I had a moment alone. We were sitting in front of the fire, the Christmas tree lights twinkling as we snuggled on the sofa, and I was transfixed by the glory that was my engagement ring. A one-and-a-half carat diamond sat in the center of an intricately woven white gold design. It made the center stone sparkle, while giving the ring a little more interest than a plain band. I realized that it matched the bracelet and I loved it.

"If you don't like the ring, we can return it," Alex offered.

"Are you high? It's like you climbed into my brain and picked my dream ring out of my head. I love it, honey," I said, and kissed him. "What I'm curious about is how you managed to keep this a surprise. I would have thought Lily would have said something."

He chuckled. "I waited until this morning to tell her anything. She's been asking if you could be her mommy and I've been putting her off until today. I wanted to talk to your dad first—"

"You talked to my dad?"

"Of course I did. Why?"

"It's just such a non-badass-biker thing to do."

He smiled. "Possibly. But it's important to you, baby."

"God, I love you, Alex."

"Back atya." He gave me a gentle squeeze. "I also talked to Kayla."

"About?" I craned my neck to look up at him.

"She's going to rent the house from me, which means I'm free to move up here when we find something."

I sat up on my knees. "So we can look for something together?" I asked, and clapped my hands.

"Yeah, baby, if that's what you want to do."

"Um, hells yeah I do. We could get married in time for you both to be up here by the school year start, and Lily and I could go to school together every day." I threw my arms around him. "This is perfect."

He laughed and pulled me onto his lap. "You've thought about this, apparently."

I smiled. "Only since the day I met you."

"In the supermarket?"

"Okay, no. Maybe just when you kissed me at the club."

Alex grinned. "I knew it in the supermarket."

"You did not."

"Baby, I saw you walkin' with Lily's hand in yours and knew you were meant to be her mom." He added in a whisper, "Bonus for me, you're fuckin' kinky in bed."

"Alex." I shifted on his lap. "Stop it."

He leaned closer to my ear. "You're wet right now, aren't you?"

I groaned and dropped my head back. "Alex," I whispered.

"Later, I'm gonna sneak into your room and fuck you, baby. I want you naked and waiting for me, yeah?"

I swallowed and nodded.

"I'm gonna eat your pussy first. And I'm gonna be real thorough. You won't speak, you won't moan, you won't touch me. I will let you come and then I'll fuck you. But again, you won't make a noise. Depending on how well you do, I'll decide if you can come. Then I'll leave you."

I licked my lips and squeezed my eyes shut.

"Okay, love birds, time for dessert," Anna said, as she moved through the room to the basement stairs.

I jumped a little, but Alex had me anchored to him, so she probably didn't notice. He smiled and kissed me, giving me a second to compose myself, before letting me off his lap. I moved through the rest of the night in a fog of arousal, while Alex seemed totally cool and collected. It didn't help that he'd find ways to whisper the things he planned to do to me once the house was asleep. Gah! I almost pulled him into the bathroom with me for a quickie, but I had to admit, this little game was fun.

My parents' house was set up essentially the way it had always been. Brock and I had our own rooms on the second floor, while Kris and Anna had shared the bonus room. This all worked until Kristen hit her teens, and she and Anna began to fight constantly. This prompted my parents to build out the basement in order to give us all a bit more space. Before my dad went into insurance sales, he'd been a contractor, so he and his brother, along with help from all of us, did the work himself.

They'd built in an entertainment room, three bedrooms (one with an attached bathroom) and another bathroom that was shared. Kris and Anna had moved downstairs back in the day, but when I moved back in, I took Kris's old room with the bathroom.

My parents kept threatening to sell and downsize, but I'd believe it when I saw it. My mom would internally combust if she didn't have enough space for everyone to feel comfortable.

By around eight, Lily couldn't keep her eyes open, so

Alex and I put her to bed in the bedroom farthest from mine. He'd be sleeping in the one in between us, or at least, that was the "plan."

We closed her door and Alex pulled me into my room, pushing me against the wall and kissing me breathless. His hand slipped under my skirt and I found my panties ripped from my body. He slid his hand between my legs and cupped me gently. "I knew you were wet."

"I can't wait until later, honey."

"You're gonna have to." He smiled slowly and stroked a finger through my wetness before removing his hand. I groaned when his tongue slid up his finger and he smiled. "Fuckin' honey, baby."

"Not fair," I rasped.

He kissed me again and then headed to my bathroom to wash his hands. I opened a bureau drawer and looked for a replacement pair of underwear, only to have him pull me away and close the drawer.

"No panties."

"Seriously?" I asked.

"Seriously." He stroked my cheek. "I want full access to your pussy for the rest of the night."

I squeezed my legs together at the thought. "This only makes me wetter, Hawk, you realize that."

"I do."

"Ohmigod, I'm going to have to walk with my knees together."

Alex laughed. "If you do that, your family will know you're not wearing panties, baby. Think about that."

"You're a butt."

He smacked mine and then led me out of the room.

FIFTEEN

Payton

I WAS NAKED and waiting, as per the instructions, and my body was primed. God, it was primed. Alex found ways to slip his hand under my skirt that were beyond stealth. The first had been in the kitchen when we were pouring drinks for everyone. We were alone, albeit only hidden from the waist down by the large kitchen island. From behind, he'd run his hand between my thighs and slipped a finger inside me before lightly touching my clit. Then he was gone.

The next time was the classic "under the table" move, where his hand slid up my thigh, his pinky connecting with me before laughing at something my brother said and looping his arm around the back of my chair. There had been several more, but thinking about them just made me crazy. I was forced to keep my expression as impassive as possible, but it grew increasingly harder as the night wore on, and all I wanted to do was get him alone.

I had to go through saying goodnight to everyone, except

Brock and Bailey who were staying the night, and then had to muddle through nightcaps and polite conversation.

I turned in as soon as I possibly could, feigning exhaustion, and sequestered myself in my bedroom to get ready for him.

Alex had kissed me at the top of the stairs and ordered, "No touching yourself."

"Well, don't make me wait."

He pulled me closer and slid his hand between my legs, leaning against my ear and whispering, "This is mine tonight. Only I touch it. Get me?"

I swallowed and nodded. He ran his finger through me again and smiled. "Good girl."

I'd walked woodenly down the basement stairs, checked in on Lily who was sound asleep, and then headed to my room.

And now I waited.

I had to leave my bed and pace a few times otherwise, I was sure I'd whip out my vibrator and take care of myself, but as frustrating as this little game was, it was also sexy as hell and I couldn't wait for Alex to join me.

I was lying on my bed, the covers partially over me when my door slid open and Alex slipped inside. He closed and locked the door, and I bit my lip. He wore a pair of pajama bottoms and wife-beater that showcased his muscular arms, and he was delicious.

He yanked off his shirt and made his way to the bed. Without a word, he threw the covers off me and settled himself between my legs. "Spread."

I spread.

And ohmigod, I was so glad I did. What that man could do with his mouth was surely illegal in several countries. I felt my body building and he smiled against me. "Come, but no noise," he whispered.

I nodded and he resumed his assault. If you have ever been forced to climax in silence, it is both almost impossible and sexier than anything I'd experienced to date. Okay, being tied to the ceiling of a boat was pretty amazing, but this was a close second. I threw my pillow over my face so that my panting breaths couldn't be heard.

Alex slipped it away and smiled down at me. "Deep breaths, baby, or you'll hyperventilate."

"I don't know if I can," I whispered.

He chuckled quietly. "Try."

I nodded and did what I could to keep from passing out.

"Good girl," he said. "You liked that."

"I *loved* that," I corrected.

Alex grinned again, climbing off the bed and removing his pj's. "All fours, Payton, edge of the mattress."

Holy crap, yes!

I moved into position and he stood behind me, running a palm down my back. "No noise."

I nodded and took a deep breath. He slid into me and I dropped my head to the mattress, face to the covers, because not making noise when he was taking me from behind seemed like an impossibility.

He reached his hand between my legs and ran a fingertip over my clit as he surged into me again and again.

"Ohmigod," I breathed into the bedding.

He slammed into me one more time and I came around him. It took him a few more thrusts to join me, but then we fell onto the bed and I was once again left without breath.

"I'm very proud of you, baby," he whispered, and slid out of me.

And then he was gone.

Okay, that part sucked. I was all for a naughty game of forbidden sex, but him leaving me right after…hell, no. I still hadn't fully caught my breath, but I washed up in the bathroom, pulled on a pair of shorts and a cami, and headed to his room. I pushed open the door to find him grinning at me from the edge of his bed.

"I was about to come to you," he said.

I slid into his arms and squeezed him as hard as I could. "Everything was amazing up until the you leaving me part. That sucked."

"Yeah, that went a little differently than I expected." He kissed my temple. "No more leaving."

"Deal." I smiled up at him. "I don't know how I'm going to sleep without you."

"I'll come sleep with you for a bit. I'll set my alarm in case I fall asleep."

"I doubt anyone will come down here, honey."

He smiled. "When your mother put us in separate rooms, baby, it sent a message."

"It's not like she doesn't know we're having sex."

"But knowing it and *knowing* it are two different things," he pointed out.

"Whatever. Come with me fiancé. We're gonna have a little more fun and then I'm going to fall asleep on you."

Alex chuckled and followed me to my room.

* * *

I woke the next morning to an empty bed, but the smell of Alex still clung to the sheets. I checked my phone and discovered it was nine a.m., so I forced myself off the mattress and dressed quickly, before looking for my fiancé. I loved saying that. He was my fiancé.

I found him at the kitchen table with Lily and my brother, and he pulled me onto his lap for a kiss. "Good morning, sleepyhead."

Lily climbed on top of me with a giggle. "Morning, Pay—Mommy."

I pulled her close, even though her hands were sticky from syrup. "Morning, baby. How did you sleep?"

"Good." She bobbed her head up and down, and then

quickly jumped off my lap so she could go back to the pan-cakes my mom had made.

"Gotta run somethin' by you, babe," Alex said. "Let's get coffee."

He patted my bottom and I climbed off his lap. In the kitchen, I poured coffee and he leaned against the counter. "I've got some club business to take care of. Not sure how long I'll be."

"It's Christmas."

Alex smiled. "Technically it's not, which means I need to take care of this."

"Can I keep Lily?"

He laughed. "Yeah, baby, if you want to. It means I don't have to drive her down to Kayla."

"Us girls always go shopping today, so I'd love for her to join us."

"That would be great," he said. "I'll leave the car seat."

"Just text me when you know when you'll be done. You're welcome to stay here, obviously, or I can drive down to your place."

He pulled his wallet out and pulled out a wad of cash…yes, a *wad*.

I pushed his hand away. "I have money, Alex."

"Babe, take the money."

"Nope, I'm good."

"Payton," he said, his voice dipped low.

"Alex." I mimicked his voice. "Put your money back in your wallet. If I want to buy something, I'll buy it. You pay for everything when we're together anyway. Now it's my chance to feel like I'm not a kept woman."

He slid his hand to my neck. "We'll play that game next time."

I shivered and smiled up at him. "Can't wait."

He leaned down and kissed me quickly and then we walked back to Lily.

"Daddy's gotta go to work, baby girl. Payton's gonna take you shopping."

"Okay, Daddy." She hugged him and then went back to her pancakes.

"Thought that would go different," Alex whispered.

I grinned. "I'll walk you out."

"Watch her, Payton. She sees something shiny and walks away and you won't hear her."

I rolled my eyes. "Wonder who she gets that from?"

He pulled open the door and smiled.

"You're not doing anything dangerous are you?" I asked.

"I'm not doin' anything I don't do every week."

"That doesn't actually answer my question."

He leaned down and kissed me. "Love you, babe."

"Love you too."

He headed to his truck and, after he handed me the car seat, I raised up on my tiptoes and gave him a kiss on the cheek. "Have a great day at work, honey."

Alex laughed and took off.

I made my way back to the kitchen to find Bailey sitting at the table with Brock and Lily. "Good morning," I said.

Bailey smiled sleepily. "Hey. What time are we leaving?"

"I think in about an hour. Anna's going to be here around eleven." I sat beside Lily and slid her hair behind an ear. "How were those pancakes?"

"Yummy."

"Make sure you tell Nana and thank her, okay?"

She grinned. "'K."

"Let's get you cleaned up and then we'll get dressed for shopping, sound good?"

Lily nodded her head and pushed away from the table.

"Go ahead and carry your plate into the kitchen and I'll rinse it off for you."

She grabbed her plate and I tried not to laugh as she gingerly carried it into the kitchen. Granted, it was kind of a big plate for a little girl, but still, cute as a button.

* * *

"Oooh, these are awesome," I said, and pulled two of the twelve-inch nutcrackers off the shelf. "They're only seven bucks."

Anna grinned. "Grab me one, please."

"And me," Mom said.

"I only have so many hands," I said with a laugh. "Lily, can you—" I glanced down and she was gone. "Crap! Where the hell did she go?"

I dropped the nutcrackers in the cart and left it where it was. Anna watched the carts while Bailey, me, and Mom went looking for Lily.

I walked down the third aisle to see her talking to a man hunkered down in front of her. I don't know why, call it my new mom intuition, but I pulled out my cell phone and snapped a photo of him. "Lily!"

"Hi Mommy."

"Come here, baby," I said, but the man rose to his feet and laid a hand on her shoulder.

"Lily and I were just getting acquainted, Payton."

"I believe you have me at a disadvantage." I held my hand out to Lily. "Come here, Lily."

"Ow," she squeaked, and I saw red.

I advanced on him. "You need to let my daughter go."

"We're not done."

"Lily, honey, close your eyes."

She did and I slammed my palm to his nose, pushing up, not enough to jam his nasal bone into his brain, but hard enough to draw blood.

"Fuck," he bellowed, but released Lily.

I grabbed her arm gently and pulled her to me.

"There you are," my mom exclaimed, and I spun to face her.

"Take Lily, Mom. I need to take care of something."

She frowned, but held her hand out to Lily. "Come with Nana, honey. We'll go find your aunties."

Lily rushed to my mom and I pulled out my phone again, video on.

"You fucking bitch," the man hissed.

"I don't know who you are, but I *will* find out and if you *ever* come near my daughter again, you'll have to deal with Hawk. No one wants to deal with Hawk, so heed my warning." I turned and walked away, hoping the people milling around didn't try to find out why I left a man bleeding from the face in the middle of the aisle.

I fired off the video and photo to both Alex and Brock, and then called Alex. "Not a good time."

"Sorry, honey, but I just sent you a photo and a video. That man hurt Lily."

"What the fuck?" he snapped. "Hold on. Be back, Booker." There was silence and then I heard a door close. "What happened?"

"I lost her for about a minute and she was talking with that man. He knew her name and mine…Lily could have told him I guess, but I don't think so."

"He hurt her?" he said, carefully, like he was holding back rage.

"He squeezed her shoulder when she tried to come to me. She's with my mom. I think he scared her more than anything."

"Fuck!"

"She's okay, honey, but you need to find out who he is."

"Fuck."

"Alex, she's okay. I've got her. You'll see the guy's face on the video…I took care of him for now. You get to do the follow-up."

"I want to talk to her."

I nodded and went back to the aisle I'd left the carts. Lily was in my mom's arms, her arms around her neck. She looked a little shaken up, but surprisingly okay.

"Daddy wants to talk to you, baby."

Mom set her down and she took the phone from me. "Hi, Daddy. I'm okay. Unh-huh. Payton bought cwackers for nuts." She smiled. "Okay."

Lily handed the phone back to me. "Hi."

"She's fine."

I smiled. "I know."

Alex sighed. "Thank you, baby. If you hadn't…well, thank you."

"You can thank me properly later."

"Promise."

"I'll let you go. I've got our girl, honey, so you find out who this bastard is and deal with him."

"Yeah."

"Love you."

"Love you too," he said, and hung up.

"Payton," my mom whispered as she pulled me away from Lily, Anna, and Bailey. "What *is* going on?"

"I don't know yet, Mom. Alex is going to find out."

"Did you do that to that man?"

"Yeah, Mom, I did."

She smiled. "Brock did a good job teaching you how to fight."

Okay, not the response I expected. I chuckled. "Yeah, he did."

"Should we get Lily home do you think?"

I shook my head. "No, I don't want her to get scared, and I think if we run home and hide, it'll worry her more."

"Whatever you think, honey."

"Thanks, Mom."

We walked back to the group and I noticed Bailey was on her phone. "Lily, can you stay with Nana and Anna for a bit? I want to show auntie Bailey something."

Lily nodded.

"I mean, it Lily. You stay with Nana. If you run off again without telling an adult, you're going on time out."

She wrinkled her nose, but nodded again.

"Mom, we'll be right back."

Bailey ended her call and followed me around the corner.

"Was that Brock?" I asked.

"Yeah, he got your texts. I guess he tried to call you, but you must have been on with Alex."

"I'll call him back." I nodded toward her purse. "Do you have your gun with you?"

Bailey grimaced. "Always, but please tell me I'm not going to need it."

I smiled. "I hope we don't. But if we do, I'll take it from you."

She let out a sigh of relief. "Thank you. I know Brock wants me to carry at all times, but I still get nervous at the shooting range. I can't imagine pointing it at an actual human being."

"It'll get better. I remember being nervous as well."

"Where's *your* gun?" she whispered.

"Locked up tight at home." I bit my lip. "I haven't had the 'I own a gun and know how to use it' conversation with Alex yet. Plus, I didn't think I'd be in a position where I'd need it, especially shopping with my family."

"Seriously."

"I'm going to call Brock really quick and then I'll find you guys."

Bailey nodded and walked away. I took a minute to fill my brother in on what happened and then rejoined my family.

SIXTEEN

Payton

ALEX WANTED NOTHING to do with the idea of me driving down to Beaverton to meet him, insisting he pick me and Lily up when he was done dealing with "club business." The problem was he wouldn't be back our way until past ten, so the new plan was to stay at my place.

I had kept Lily busy with helping to break down the tree and put away ornaments. We also helped my mom with boxing up all of our decorations, new and old. I put a very tired Lily to bed around seven and joined my parents in the family room to watch a movie. They went to bed as soon as the movie was over, but I chose to wait up for Alex.

Brock had already been by to take down more information about the incident at the store, but also, I suspected, to check on Bailey. He and Dallas were on duty, and I think he was glad he had a legitimate excuse to make sure she was safe. Bailey left with Brock so he could drop her at Macey's for the night.

I heard the front door close just past ten and dropped my head onto the back of the couch to receive the most delicious upside-down kiss from Alex. Spiderman had nothin' on him. "Hi, honey."

"Hey," he whispered, and joined me on the sofa, pulling me onto his lap and holding me close.

I smiled and wrapped my arms around his shoulders. "We're okay."

He kissed my neck and nodded. "I talked to Brock."

"What did he say?"

"They followed you."

"Followed us?" I gasped. "From *here*?"

Alex nodded. "Do you remember seeing anything?"

"No." I dropped my head to his shoulder. "Ohmigod, Alex. I saw nothing weird. I'm so sorry."

"Baby, it's not your fault. They knew what they were doing. Your brother's doing some checking."

"But I led them right to us."

"No, you didn't. I did."

I sat up to meet his eyes. "What does that mean?"

"The fucker you hit? He's Jenny's new man."

"Shit, really?"

He sighed with a nod. "I haven't mentioned the issues with her since she came to the club, but she's been fuckin' makin' my life hell."

"Why didn't you tell me?"

"Because I don't want her shit to touch you."

"But it *is* touching me, honey, and I'd kind of like to know what I'm up against." He shook his head, so I cupped his cheeks and frowned. "Tell me. I can help."

"Babe," he whispered.

"Alex, nothing you tell me will make me stop loving you. Nothing will make me want to leave you. The only problem we'll ever have in that regard is if you keep me out of the loop." He closed his eyes so I kissed each one and then his lips. "I love you Alex James. Always and forever."

He dropped his forehead to mine and kissed me gently.

"Tell me," I said again.

"She's trying to get Lily. I haven't figured out exactly why yet, because I know she doesn't actually want her, but she's fuckin' gettin' dirty." He stroked my back. "Mack's got the legal shit sorted, she doesn't have a legal leg to stand on, which is why I think she's tryin' to get to me through you."

I scowled. "This chick's like a venereal disease…she just keeps coming back."

He nodded.

"What do you mean by legal stuff?" I asked. "Is there anything I should know?"

"She signed away her parental rights when she walked out on Lily, and she's been gone too long to contest them…not that she could have back then, but I might have agreed to giving her visiting rights if she'd come back."

I frowned. "I thought you didn't know where she was."

"I didn't. Booker and Mack handled it so I'd have plausible deniability. Booker can find anyone anywhere, and Mack called in my favor so I didn't have to. He did it under the guise of club business so Booker couldn't refuse."

I rolled my eyes. "You two are almost as bad as women."

He smiled. "You might be right."

"So what happens now?"

"For now, you and Lily don't go anywhere without me."

I chuckled. "You're hilarious."

"I'm fuckin' serious, Payton. You are never without me."

"Well, then you better get this solved before school starts, otherwise that's going to be impossible."

"No it won't."

"Um, yeah, it will, Hawk. How are you going to take me to and from school every day when we live over an hour away from each other…more with traffic?"

"I'll figure it out."

"*Or*, you let me take care of me," I argued. "I understand if you feel more comfortable being with me when Lily's around, but I own a gun, I know how to use it, and as you could see by the video, I know how to hit someone hard enough to hurt them."

"Let me make something clear." His eyes darkened and his hand slid to my neck. "The gun conversation is going to have to wait, but you are not gonna fuckin' 'take care of yourself,' Payton. At least, not in this situation. Jenny's fuckin' crazy and I won't have you caught in the middle."

"You're overreacting."

"I don't fuckin' care, Payton. It's not up for discussion."

"Ohmigod, Hawk. 'It's not up for discussion'? Who are you? My dad?" I pushed off his lap. "I'm going to bed."

"Payton."

"Goodnight." I left him sitting on the sofa and (admittedly) I kind of hoped he choked on his alpha male bullshit.

* * *

I had been in bed for almost an hour (not sleeping), when my door opened, and Alex walked in. He wore pajama bottoms and nothing else, but I forced myself to ignore my body (mostly because it was suddenly horny), and closed my eyes. The dip of the bed had me opening them again and I found myself face-to-face with Alex. "What do you want?"

His answer was to run his lips across my neck, and then his mouth was on mine and I was being pulled on top of him as his hand slid into my hair. I turned my head, breaking the kiss, and laid my hand over his mouth. "Green."

Alex sighed and rolled me so we were facing each other. "I just want you safe."

"I get it, honey. I do. And I appreciate that…to a point." I stroked his check. "I don't really know why I'm mad, honestly. I watch Bailey and Macey and see how crazy they get with Brock and Dallas, and I think I just…"

"Overreacted?"

I slapped his chest. "Can we both admit to a little over-reaction?"

He slipped his hand under my cami and stroked my back. "I'm not overreacting."

"This is not the way to get back into my bed, Hawk."

"In case you didn't notice, I *am* back in your bed." He moved his hand to cup my breast.

I bit the inside of my cheek to keep from arching into his touch. "Can we just talk for a second?"

He moved his hand to my back again. "If you'll give me until the end of your break to be with you every second, then I'll pull back when you go back to work."

"How will you get this sorted if you're with me every second?"

"Fuck me, Payton. Just give me this."

"Daddy?" Lily called, and Alex was out of the bed and at the door in seconds.

"Hey, baby girl." He walked out of the room, returning with her in his arms. "You have a bad dream?"

Lily nodded, sniffling into his neck.

I held my arms out. "Want to sleep in here tonight?"

"We'll all sleep in here," Alex said.

Lily smiled through her tears and Alex set her on the bed before closing the door. I held the covers up and Lily climbed between them. She wrapped her arms around my waist and snuggled close, Alex sandwiched her in and kissed me, then her. "Love you, baby girl."

"Wuv you too, Daddy." She lifted her head and kissed my cheek. "'Night, Mama."

"Night, baby. I love you."

"Wuv you, too, Payton."

I smiled at Alex and slid my arm around his waist. He did the same and we gave Lily a protective little enclosure to keep her safe.

"We'll talk more tomorrow," he whispered.

I nodded and he kissed me again.

My last coherent thought was how amazing it was that such a tiny little body could produce so much heat. I ended up throwing the blankets off my legs in an effort not to burn up.

* * *

I woke to an empty bed again and debated on getting up, but the pull of Alex and the fact I got him for the next week kind of won out.

I dressed quickly and made my way upstairs to find him. Lily was at the kitchen island, crayon in hand, concentrating on the coloring book in front of her. My mom was closing up the dishwasher as I walked in.

I kissed Lily's head and smiled. "Morning, honey."

"Hi," she said, and smiled.

"Coffee's in the pot, honey," Mom said.

"Thanks." I grabbed a cup and then leaned next to Lily. "I love your picture."

"Fank you."

"Where's Daddy?"

She didn't look up as she said, "On the woof."

"He's helping Dad and Brock with the lights," my mom clarified.

Brock and Bailey must have come by earlier. "Where's Bailey?"

"She went upstairs to take a nap. I think she's coming down with a cold," Mom said.

"Ew, no fun," I said. "I'll go check on Alex."

I opened the slider and peeked outside. Alex was up on the ladder, tugging at a string of lights, his eyes narrowed in concentration. I bit my lip, our argument the night before quickly forgotten at the sight of jeans slung low on his hips, and his T-shirt sliding up revealing his flat stomach.

"Hi honey."

"Hey, babe," he said, continuing to focus on the job at hand.

177

"Hawk, I'm going to drop down a string," my dad called.

When did Dad start calling him 'Hawk'?

"Ready," Alex said, and craned his head up.

Lights slid into his hand and he dropped them to the deck.

"Do you need help?" I asked.

"Not yet, babe. Lily okay?" He still didn't look at me as he went back to the clips on the gutters.

"Yep, she's coloring." I bit my lip. "Gordon asked if we want to talk about houses at some point so he can pull a few listings for us to look at."

"Today?"

"Or whenever."

He looked at me…*finally*.

"Can we talk about it when we're done here, babe?" I nodded and he smiled. "You sleep okay?"

"Yes. You?"

"Not really. Kept getting kicked by little feet."

I tried not to chuckle. "Uh-oh."

"Hawk, lights comin' your way." This came from my brother.

"Ready," he said and caught another strand as it slid down.

"I'll leave you to it."

"Thanks, babe," Alex said, and I let myself back inside.

Lily was still coloring and I slid her hair behind her ear and lifted her chin. "Are you hungry?"

She shook her head. "Huh-uh."

"Are you sure? I'm going to make some peanut butter toast."

"Nana made me some aweddy."

My mom turned from the sink. "Yeah, Nana's got it all covered."

I grinned. "Thanks, Mom."

"I'm heading over to Kristen's in a bit," Mom asked. "Anything you want me to take?"

"No, I'm good." I dropped a slice of bread into the toaster. "I guess I need to wait for Alex to get off the roof before we plan our day. Is there anything you want to do, Lily?"

She settled her chin in her hand. "Umm, can we go to the movies?"

"Maybe," I said. "I'll ask Daddy and we'll see if something appropriate is playing."

"What does appwopi-it mean?"

"Basically, it means we'll find a movie that you are old enough to see."

She nodded and smiled. "I'm going potty." She climbed down off the stool and headed to the bathroom.

Alex opened the slider a few seconds later and frowned. "Where's Lily?"

"Bathroom," I said, and slathered peanut butter on my toast.

He said nothing and left the room, returning with Lily and lifting her back on the stool. I raised an eyebrow in annoyance at him, but he ignored me.

"Lily would like to see a movie today."

"No," he said, and grabbed a glass from the cabinet.

"Why not?" I challenged.

"Lily, why don't you come help Nana for a minute," Mom said, and led Lily out of earshot.

He slid his glass under the water maker of the fridge. "Neither of you is leaving this house, Payton."

"Surely going to a movie isn't going to put us in danger."

"You said you'd give me the week," he reminded me.

"To be all up in my grill, but not to keep me sequestered at home!"

Alex shrugged. "Until I know exactly what I'm up against, you're here."

"How are we going to look at houses?"

"We're not."

"What about the New Year's party at Macey's?"

He shook his head.

"Are you kidding me?" I snapped. "I'm not missing my best friend's annual party, Hawk."

"I'm not arguing with you on this subject, babe. Accept it and move on."

"Bite me." I stormed out of the room and downstairs.

* * *

Hawk

I stood in the kitchen and watched her leave. I wanted to fuckin' kill Jenny… more so than before. I had no idea how Payton and I would move past this, but I had to keep them safe or I'd never forgive myself.

My phone buzzed, and I reached into my pocket, pulling it out. "Hey, Kay."

"Are you sitting down?" she asked.

"Not currently, no. Why?"

"Mike called last night—"

"Why the hell are you taking his calls?"

Mike was Kayla's ex, and not only did he step out on her, he was a major douchebag in general.

"Just listen," she stressed. "I didn't take his call. He left me a voicemail and I called him back because of what he told me."

I sighed. "Yeah, and what did the fucker say?"

"He was at *The Pink Fox*, you know, the strip club in Gresham?"

"Can't say I do, but go on."

"Anyway, it's run by some Russian mob guys, and they offer services that go further than lap dances. Mike was there, shocker, but guess who one of the prostitutes was?"

"I'm on the edge of my seat, Kay," I droned sarcastically.

"Jenny."

"Come again?"

"Jenny. She was totally strung out, topless, and up for

180

anything. Mike videotaped her screwing one of his work buddies and sent it to me. Gross, but he thought you'd want it."

I leaned against the counter. "And why would he think I'd want it?"

"Because she talked about you on the video. Just watch it. You'll see. I emailed it to you."

"Okay, sister. Thanks."

"Sure."

"You okay?" I asked.

"Is it wrong to admit I don't miss you?" she asked. "I miss Lily, but I have to say, not waking up at the crack of dawn is kind of nice."

I laughed. "Well, you got the week to enjoy it."

"I bet Payton will love that."

"You'd think."

"What did you do?" she challenged. "Did you have a rational conversation with her, or did you go all Tarzan on her?"

"Coulda been somewhere in between."

"Love you, bro, but you're an idiot."

"I'm not having this conversation with you, Kay."

Kayla laughed. "Okay, okay, but if you drive her away again, I will kill you."

My heart dropped at the thought. "I won't."

"Okay, gotta jet. Talk to you later."

"'Bye."

I hung up and loaded my email. Brock and Chuck walked in just as the video loaded, so I pressed pause. "Need anything?"

Chuck shook his head. "We're done."

I nodded.

"Where's Pay?" Brock asked.

"Downstairs I think," I said.

"I'm going to clean up," Chuck said, and headed out of the kitchen.

"You okay?" Brock asked, and grabbed a glass of water.

I sighed and shook my head. "I'm missin' somethin'."

"With the Jenny situation?"

"Yeah."

"Want to map it out?"

"Kayla sent me a video." I stepped closer to Brock and pressed play.

When the video ended, Brock shook his head. "She's fucked up."

"Yeah. She was a wacko before Lily, but add drugs to the mix, and she's… I don't know. Fuckin' gone."

"Where was that taken?"

"*The Pink Fox*."

"Shit, really?" Brock said.

I nodded. "Why?"

"We busted a human trafficking ring a while ago. The bastards who ran the operation owned that club. Among others."

"Who's running it now?"

"On paper? A guy named Brian Nolan."

"None of this makes any fuckin' sense."

"Forward it to me, I'll look into it," Brock offered.

I nodded and fired it off to Brock just as Payton walked into the kitchen, rinsed her plate, and dumped it in the dishwasher… all without speaking. Brock raised an eyebrow at me, waved his phone, and left the room, also without speaking.

When Payton moved to leave, I grabbed her arm and pulled her against me. "I know you're pissed."

"You're a freakin' genius, handsome. Well done."

"I'm doin' this to keep you safe, Payton. Fuckin' cut me some slack."

"I might be a little more inclined to 'cut you some slack' if you weren't so beat your chest, I am man, you are woman about it. I also might be a little more inclined to cut you some slack if you gave me some credit." Payton pushed away from me. "But since you don't seem willing to do that, then we're at an impasse, bub."

I pulled her to me again.

"Hawk," she snapped.

I wrapped my arms around her waist and slid one hand into her hair, tugging it gently so she'd drop her head back. "Baby, I don't know how bad this threat is. I'm feeling a little overwhelmed that you and Lily might be in danger, so, if you don't mind, could we just hang here at your parents' place until I get a better read on the situation?"

I smiled when her eyes narrowed, mostly because she was trying to keep from smiling. "You're a butt," she retorted.

"So I've been told." I cupped her ass. "Love you, baby."

She rolled her eyes. "You should. I'm amazing."

I leaned forward and kissed her nose. "I will make this up to you. I promise."

Payton's body relaxed and she sighed. "I want boat time… with play."

"Fuck me," I whispered as I kissed her neck. "Don't say shit like that in the middle of your parents' kitchen."

She grinned. "Payback's a bitch, handsome."

"Daddy!" Lily exclaimed as she rushed into the kitchen. "Can we go to a movie? Pweese?"

I released Payton and hunkered down in front of my daughter. "Not today, baby girl, but I bet we can find a movie to watch downstairs. All three of us. What do you think?"

"Can we have popcorn?"

"Of course we can have popcorn," Payton said.

I smiled up at her and mouthed, 'thank you.'

Payton smiled back and headed to the pantry.

Payton

I WAS WRITHING against Alex as his mouth licked, sucked, and generally made me crazy. My legs were over his shoulders and he held my hips still so I had limited movement, while he ate me. I was enjoying the process, but when he slid two fingers inside of me, I came so fast, I groaned in frustration. "Damn it, honey, I was enjoying that."

He chuckled as he climbed over me. "I have never once heard a woman complain about fuckin' comin' until you, Payton."

"Well, I happen to like your mouth on me and it's always far too short."

"Unless I'm takin' too long and you want my cock," he countered, and slid into me.

I arched my hips. "Well, yes. That's true, but you should be able to read my mind by now."

"Want me to stop and go back to what I was doin'?"

I grabbed his arms. "Don't you dare."

Alex surged into me as he covered my mouth with his. He braced himself with an arm on the mattress beside me and cupped my breast, rolling a nipple between his fingers. Before I could climax, he came, falling on top of me, his breath coming in pants. Within seconds, he pulled out of me and slid his fingers in, thumbing my clit while he finished me off. I drew my knees together and rocked against his hand, clenching around his fingers as I came.

I grinned and craned my neck to kiss him. "You're forgiven."

He wrapped an arm around me and pulled me close. "It won't be for long."

"You don't actually know that, honey."

"Your brother's helping."

"He is?"

Alex nodded. "I think it's bigger than just Jenny wanting Lily."

"Well, that changes things a bit."

"Yeah, it does."

I dropped my head against his shoulder and kissed his chest. "Can we at least look at a few houses? Together? I want our own space."

"Give me a couple of days, yeah? Just need to see what Brock can find and then we'll go from there."

"Well, you better keep me and Lily occupied, then."

He grinned and cupped my breast. "Promise."

* * *

Hawk

Two days later, I left the safety of the Williams' home, but only because Brock stationed a plain car on the street. I was meeting Brock and Dallas at the Portland FBI office and, after a little prodding, was able to get Payton to agree not to leave the house. She was getting antsy, as was Lily, but it couldn't be helped.

I arrived and was ushered by Brock into a private office. Dallas shook my hand and they introduced me to Jaxon Quinn, another member of their close-knit team.

"We know who was at the store," Brock started, and slipped a file toward me. "His name is Arseny Bekhterev and he's the baby brother of Boris and Vasily, whom we busted in the human trafficking sting. The family has been lying low, but it would appear Arseny has been working quite quickly to build the family business up again."

I glanced through the file. "So, how does Jenny fit into all of this?"

"Well, according to Jenny, who is currently in custody and going through withdrawals in a secure medical facility, he is her pimp."

"Fuckin' bitch got into prostitution?"

"Not on purpose. She met Arseny, fell in love, and he has been turning her out ever since he got her hooked on heroin. What we've discovered, however, is that she has done some very stupid things, including stealing dope, and they want payback."

"Which means?" I pressed.

Brock grimaced. "Lily."

My blood ran cold. "Are you saying she's offering Lily up as payment?"

Dallas nodded.

"What the fuck!" I stood, slamming my chair back against the wall. "Take me to Jenny. I'm gonna kill the fuckin' whore."

"That's not gonna happen, Hawk," Brock said.

"I can't believe she'd sell my…" I dragged my hands through my hair. "Fuck!"

"We're on it, brother." Brock waved to my chair. "But there's more."

"Fuck me," I whispered and took my seat again.

"Ashley is your club president's daughter, right?"

I nodded.

"Well, she got a little too close to Boris's son, Vadim, and he felt humiliated when Ashley dumped him. Jenny said the family wants to bring down the club."

"Shit." I dragged my hands down my face. "Ash has been gettin' death threats ever since she cut the guy loose, but he's disappeared."

"Well, yes and no," Dallas said.

"What do you mean?"

"He has a few aliases," Brock provided. "They all do."

"Makes sense," I said.

"You may want someone to watch her," Brock said.

I nodded. "She's already covered."

"Good," Brock said. "Let's figure out what we can do in the meantime."

Before we could delve into anything, a knock at the door brought a young agent, his face set with concern.

"Brock, Smith and Flores got an issue at the house."

Brock and Dallas stood and left the room while Jaxon picked up the office phone. I grabbed my cell and dialed Payton, my heart in my throat.

"Hi honey," Payton said.

"You and Lily okay?"

"Yeah, why?"

"Fuck," I said, my breath leaving my body.

"What's wrong?"

I rubbed my forehead. "Somethin's going on at the house. Not sure what yet. Do me a favor and stay close to Lily. Can you get your gun and have it holstered and on you?"

"Sure. Honey, you're scaring me. What's going on?"

"Don't know yet. I'm on my way home, so just stay put." I pulled my keys out of my pocket. "Love you."

"Love you too."

I hung up and rushed out of the room. Jaxon was still on

the phone, talking to someone internally, but I couldn't wait for information. I needed to get home.

"Hawk, wait up," Brock called, and jogged to catch up to him. "I'll walk out with you."

I pressed the elevator button, my stomach churning with fear. "What did you find out?"

"Pizza delivery. Guy looked off, so one of my guys patted him down. He was carrying. A little more investigation found the real pizza guy bound, gagged, and unconscious in his car a couple blocks away."

"Fuck me," I breathed out as we stepped into the elevator.

"It's one of Arseny's guys, but he's in custody. I sent another car, and two guys will stay in front while the other two do a sweep. We've got this."

I nodded, but wouldn't feel better until I got back to the house and could physically hold my girls.

"Payton should carry at all times," Brock continued. "Not sure what she should do at school, but we've got a week, so we'll sort it out when the time comes."

I nodded again.

"They're safe. Bailey's there as well and she says they're fine. My parents left an hour ago, so the house is locked up and the alarm is on." Brock stared at the wall. "Bailey knows the drill, as does Payton."

"I hear you, but until they're in front of me and I can touch them…"

Brock grimaced. "I get it."

"You comin' home?"

Brock shook his head. "I trust my team. I need to find out what else this bastard is into."

I nodded and stepped out of the elevator with a chin lift to Brock as he headed back upstairs. I pulled out my phone again. Brock might trust his team, but I would only trust my family to my brothers.

Payton

I had been pacing the house for what felt like forever, occasionally peeking outside to see if I could see anything. I saw a man in a pizza uniform being led away in handcuffs and was irritated that our dinner had been destroyed…that was until Alex called. Then I was glad our dinner was the only thing that met its death in that moment.

At about five thirty, I heard motorcycle pipes, and glanced outside to see a million bikers driving up to my parents' house. Okay, a million might be an over exaggeration, but there were a lot. I recognized Booker and Mack by name, a few others I recognized by sight, but just as many were strangers to me. Lily came running into the foyer from the family room where she and Bailey were watching a movie, and she smooshed her face to the window. "Uncle Mack is here. And Booker!"

She reached for the doorknob, but I held her back. "We need to wait a bit, honey. I don't know if it's safe yet."

"But thewa dogs, Payton. They always keep me safe."

I smiled. Her absolute faith in these men was adorable. "I know, baby, but with Daddy not here, I need to make sure first, okay?"

She sighed. "Okay, Mama."

"If you want to check it out, I'll wait here with Lily," Bailey said, joining us.

I nodded and pulled open the door, making my way toward the group of some of the best looking men on the planet. Even the feds were gorgeous in a buttoned up, official kind of way. Of course, I knew them somewhat as they worked with my brother, but only in a casual capacity.

"Hey, babe," Mack said, and gave me a chin lift as he approached with Booker.

"Hi guys. Did Hawk call in the cavalry?"

Booker chuckled. "Somethin' like that."

"There's a little girl dying to see her uncles. Do you want to come in?"

"We're gonna wait for Hawk," Mack said.

"Oh, okay."

I turned to leave but Mack caught my arm. "Where you goin'?"

I nodded toward José Flores, one of the agents. "I was going to say hi. I'll be right back."

"Hawk wants you inside, Payton," Booker said.

"And I will be…as soon as I say hi."

"Don't think that's what he meant," Mack countered.

"I know these guys, Mack," I said, keeping the irritation from my voice as much as possible. "It's all good."

I'd barely managed to say hi to the men before Alex pulled his truck into the driveway. He looked worried as he stepped out of the truck and walked toward me, but when he caught my eye, he looked pissed. I forced myself not to roll my eyes as I closed the distance and met him halfway.

"You're supposed to be inside," he hissed.

"I was until about ten minutes ago. Lily's dying to see her uncles, but I told her I wanted to check things out first."

"Where's your gun?"

"In my holster at my back," I said.

"Is it loaded?"

I scoffed. "Are you serious?"

"Yeah."

"Ohmigod, Hawk, this isn't my first rodeo. Of *course* it's loaded."

He slipped his hand to my neck and thumbed my pulse. "You're okay."

I wrapped an arm around his waist. "Yes, honey, we're both okay."

His body finally relaxed and he leaned down to kiss me quickly. I smiled up at him. "That's the most appropriate way to greet me, husband-to-be."

Alex chuckled and kissed me again.

"Okay, we need to let Lily out," I said. "She's been really patient, but she's missing you."

Alex scanned the area and then nodded, so I waved to Bailey and the front door flew open just in time for the little flurry of blonde to make a mad dash for Alex. "Daddy!"

He bent at the waist and caught Lily, lifting her and hugging her tightly. "Hey, baby girl."

"Owa pizza didn't come."

"I heard," he said. "I'll have a recruit pick another one up, yeah?"

"Okay, Daddy. Can I get down now?"

Alex lowered her to the ground and she made a beeline for Mack who lifted her the same way Alex had before hugging her and handing her off to Booker who swung her up in the air.

"Yo, Flea," Alex called.

A young man who looked about twelve, but must have been at least eighteen, came jogging up to us. "Yeah, boss."

"I need you to get pizzas. Two cheese, large combo, pepperoni."

"No problem."

I reached out my hand and smiled. "I'm Payton."

He shook it, his grin wide. "Flea."

"Nice to meet you."

He gave me a chin lift and went off to find food.

"Mama, can Uncle Mack stay?" Lily patted my leg and smiled up at me, her hand firmly in Mack's.

I chuckled. "Of course he can."

"Yay. Come on, Mack. Let's watch Fwozen." She tugged him away and he looked back at us helplessly.

"So, his appeal isn't just to the adult female population," I mused.

Alex raised an eyebrow. "What the fuck, Payton?"

I chuckled. "Not my type, honey. Don't worry."

"Better." He smiled and kissed me quickly before turning

toward the crowd. "Booker. Inside."

Booker gave him a salute, left the man he was standing with, and followed us inside.

"Should I send food out?" I asked.

"Nah, they're splittin' up shifts," Alex said. "When the dust settles, we can go from there."

"Okay. I should probably call my parents and warn them that there's a biker gang in front of their house."

"You do that. I'll grab the beer from my truck and talk to my brothers real quick."

I nodded and dialed my mom.

The rest of the night was shared with Mack, Booker, Dani (who came with Macey and Dallas), Brock and Bailey, and my parents. I have to give my parents credit. They welcomed these men into their home having never met them, and made them feel like part of the family. I got the distinct impression Mack didn't want to leave, and I think my mom would have been fine with that.

EIGHTEEN

Payton

THE SATURDAY BEFORE school started up again, Alex was wound up tighter than a spring. He'd agreed to attend Dallas and Macey's annual New Year's party the week before, but I think it was partly because pretty much every man, and a few women, were armed and able to defend me should anything happen. Lily was with my parents, still being guarded by two agents, so he "allowed" the outing.

The threat had not been "eliminated," so he hadn't slept the night before, concerned about being split between me and Lily. We'd looked at a couple of houses that week, but nothing really fit, so Gordon had suggested building. Our plan was to look at a couple of model homes in the area on Sunday.

After dinner, we spent time with Lily and then put her to bed. This gave us some precious time alone and we took drinks into the game room and sat down to talk.

"Can you take time off?" Alex asked.

"No, honey. I just had two weeks. Not to mention the time I took when Kris was in the hospital." I stroked his cheek. "I'm fine, Alex. I'll have an escort to and from school. Brock's also spoken with the principal, so he knows I'll be armed. My gun and holster are small, so no one else will know. I'm covered."

He shook his head. "I don't like you being up here without me."

"Well, you can always stay here. I know it's not the ideal situation, but Mom offered to watch Lily while we look for a preschool just in case you want to move sooner."

"I don't want to do that to your parents, babe."

"Do you have a better plan?" I challenged.

"Fuck," he whispered.

"Look, I get that you're not used to taking help, but they're offering. You've been around long enough to know that it's not offered with strings. My parents do it because they love us. You too, honey. It's unconditional."

"I know."

"So, let's plan to hang up here for a while. Who knows? We could find a house tomorrow and then some real planning can happen and we'll all feel more settled." I sipped my wine. "Who's with Kayla?"

"Buzz."

I'd met Buzz at a club night…he had been one of Booker's recruits but was now a full patch member.

"Well, she's protected, I'm protected, Lily's protected. We're all covered and you don't have to split yourself in two trying to juggle it all if you stay up here."

He sipped his beer and stared at the wall.

"You have to let us love you, honey. We're kind of rabid when people don't." One side of his mouth twitched up and I smiled.

"Salvation," he whispered.

"Hmm?"

He faced me, sliding his hand to my pulse. "You're my salvation, Payton."

"Honey, don't say that," I said. "Only God can be anyone's salvation."

"You light my path, then." Alex smiled. "Never in a million years did I ever think I'd find someone who could love me…not the way you love me. You humble me."

"I feel the same way about you, honey. I have never felt love the way you give it." I leaned into his hand. "I'm just glad you feel at least a little of what I feel for you."

He rose to his feet and took my wine. "Come with me."

I didn't hesitate, following him back to my room. Once inside, Alex set our drinks on my bureau and closed the door, locking it behind us. He stepped into my closet and pulled a box down from the ledge, setting it on the bed.

"I bought something for you." Lifting a chain out of the box, he smiled. "These are nipple clamps. We can tighten them as we go or loosen them if it doesn't work."

I shivered. "I love it when you…"

He chuckled. "I know you do. Sometimes I'm afraid I'll hurt you though. This means you have the power."

I grinned and pulled off my shirt, unclasped my bra, and let them both fall to the floor. "Show me."

"Fuck me," he breathed. "I love how much you love sex."

"I love sex with you. There's a difference."

He kissed me and then rolled my nipples between his fingers before securing each clamp and tightening the little screw. "How's that?"

"More," I said, my body already on fire.

He tightened them more and I groaned, reaching for his jeans and undoing the fly. I slid my hand under his boxer briefs and wrapped my hand around his already hardening cock. "Fuck me."

"Let's make this last a little, huh?" He tugged gently on the chain between the clamps and I shook my head, pushing my jeans and panties from my hips.

"Screw that," I said, grabbing his hand and guiding it between my legs. "Feel."

"Beautiful," he whispered, and kissed me.

Lifting me onto the bed, he laid his palm to my chest and held me where he wanted me, kneeling between my legs and covering my core with his mouth. I squirmed against his mouth and he raised his head with a frown. "If you can't stay still, I'm gonna tie you to the bed."

I licked my lips, my breath leaving my body. "Tie me."

His eyes widened and then he grinned, stepping off the bed, and heading back into my closet. He returned with two of my robe sashes and ran the end of one across my belly. "Head on the pillows, baby."

I shifted so my head was up by the headboard.

"Slide down a bit."

I slid down and he took a nipple, clamp and all, in his mouth. He pressed the clamp tighter with his teeth and I felt the heat pool between my legs. He tied one hand to the post and then the other. I was suddenly glad I hadn't swapped the guest room bed with the one I'd bought when I'd moved in with Macey. My designer headboard wasn't conducive to kinky sex. Something I'd need to think about for the future.

"Too tight?" he asked.

I shook my head, and he pushed off his jeans and knelt between my legs again. This time, he lifted my hips and slid into me, falling over me and covering my mouth with his. I wrapped my legs around him, the only way I could touch him.

He broke the kiss with a grin, sliding out of me and then in again slowly. "Put your right leg higher around my waist, I'm going to roll you slightly."

I did as he directed and he tilted me enough that my arm wasn't hyper-extended, but it opened my upper body a bit more to him. As he rocked into me, he tugged on the chain between my clamps and I hissed with need. He was going far too slow. I lifted my left leg so I could control my lower body and arched against him.

He tugged on the chain again, sending a shot of desire between my legs again. "Greedy pussy."

"God, yes," I breathed. "Please, baby, don't go slow."

He cupped my bottom and squeezed. "You want it harder?"

"Yes," I panted.

He smacked me and I threw my head back with a sigh. For the next several minutes, he tugged, slapped, and drove into me while I came apart in his arms. He rolled me onto my back again and slammed into me over and over again, his final thrust combined with pulling the chain down and I shattered.

Alex released me from my ties and I wrapped my arms around his neck and sobbed into his chest.

"Honey, did I hurt you?" he whispered, pulling me close.

"No. It was amazing," I whispered, hiccupping as I spoke. "Oh, my *God*, it was amazing."

He chuckled and held me tighter. "I love you, Payton."

I dropped my head back so I could meet his eyes. "I can tell."

Alex thumbed my tears away and kissed me gently. "I can't wait to make babies with you."

I chuckled. "Oh, yeah, babies. We haven't had that conversation yet."

He removed one clamp, sucking gently on my nipple, then did the same to the other. "How do they feel?"

"Like that's going to be something regular."

Alex laughed and climbed from the bed. "We'll branch out to other toys later."

"I want something spectacular for our honeymoon."

"Done." He put the clamps back in the box and secured them on the shelf again.

"How many kids do you want?" I asked.

"As many as you want to give me," he said, and

stretched out on the bed again.

I rolled onto his chest and kissed his neck. "Good answer."

He grinned. "I think I'd like a couple more. I like the idea of doing it *with* someone this time around."

"That all sounds good to me."

Alex pulled the covers around us and settled his hand on my bottom. "Are you excited about tomorrow?"

"Possibly building a home less than five minutes from my parents? Yes. Does that make me weird?"

"No, that doesn't make you weird…other things make you weird, but not that."

I grinned up at him. "Bite me."

"Again?" He pushed me onto my back. "Babe, you're gonna wear me out."

I chuckled as he shimmied under the blankets and kissed my stomach. He kissed one breast and then the other before pulling me against him again. "We should probably talk about how you want to handle the house situation."

"What do you mean?"

"I think you should buy it, then I think we should have a pre-nup that states we leave with whatever we came with."

I pushed away from him and sat up on my knees. "Excuse me?"

"Don't get upset, baby. I'm trying to protect you."

"From *what*?"

"In case we don't work out," he said.

Out loud. He said the dumbest thing on the fucking planet out *loud.*

I pointed to the door. "Get out."

"Payton."

"No, get out, Hawk. If you're ready for this marriage to be over before it's even started, then you better get used to sleeping on the sofa or guest room, or bathtub. I don't care. Just get out."

He let out a sigh. "Can we start over?"

"I don't know, can you get your head out of your ass before we do?"

Alex grinned. "My reasoning is pure, baby, I promise."

"I'm marrying you, Alex. You're marrying me. What's mine is yours and vice-versa. I don't want or need a prenup." I crossed my arms. "Besides, if divorce is something we discuss, I will be living off of your life insurance policy shortly after that conversation."

"You think you'll get away with it, huh?"

"Not a hair or a fiber, handsome. I will make sure of it."

He dropped his head back and laughed. "Fuck me, I love you."

I wrinkled my nose to keep from smiling. "Flattery will get you—"

My breath left my body in a "whoosh" as he threw me onto my back and kissed me before sliding his hands to my sides and tickling the shit out of me.

"I'm going to pee!" I squealed.

He grinned and tickled me again. This went on for several seconds before he let me up for air.

"We are never breaking up," I said, emphatically.

"We're never breaking up."

"Say it again," I demanded.

He grinned. "We're never breaking up."

"I need you to mean it, Alex, because if you don't feel the same way I do, this won't work."

"I'm gettin' used to being loved, babe. You gotta give me a minute."

I cupped his face. "You have fifty-eight more seconds."

"Okay, done."

I chuckled. "You're lucky you're cute."

"Do you want to watch a movie, or do you want to play some more?"

"Um, I want to watch a movie and then I want to play some more, duh."

Alex laughed and kissed me again. "Your wish is my

command."

* * *

"We found a house!" I shouted as Alex and I walked into my parents' house the next day.

"Back here, honey," Mom called.

I headed to the kitchen and Lily reached her arms up for a hug. "Did you find my room?"

"When the house is built, you get to pick your very own room and Daddy will paint it whatever color you want."

"First, we need to get qualified," Alex pointed out. "And then we can go from there."

I laid the brochure out on the island. "Four bedrooms plus a den, three and a half bathrooms, almost three-thousand square feet, it'll be perfect for us."

"It looks beautiful, honey," Mom said.

The rest of the day was spent planning and dreaming. Since the weather was mild, Lily got to run off some energy in the backyard, and then the rest of the kids arrived with their parents for our bi-monthly Sunday dinner. As we sat at the dining room table, I smiled at Alex and leaned over to kiss him. "Life's pretty freakin' perfect, huh?"

He chuckled. "So it would seem."

"I love you."

Alex linked his fingers with mine. "Love you too, baby."

I focused back on the conversation at hand and let myself bask in my glorious life of love and happiness...I had no idea how quickly things could change.

Payton

THE WEDNESDAY OF my second week back at work, I packed up my desk and headed out of school, my mind on Alex. We'd gotten the paperwork signed for our loan application and been approved, found a preschool for Lily, at least temporarily, and everything appeared to be going our way. I couldn't wait to start our new journey together. And on top of the house stuff, the wedding plans would start this weekend. Life was still perfect.

Alex and I were heading to the builder's office tonight to pick options and appliances, then it was off to the carpet place tomorrow to pick tile, carpet and such. As I walked out the front doors, I was met by a new agent, Kyle Cobb, and he smiled in greeting.

"Hey, Kyle."

"Payton. How was your day?"

"Not bad. Yours?"

"Good," he said. "We have a few leads, so that's a positive."

"Awesome," I said. "Does that mean you guys are close to shutting this thing down?"

Kyle didn't get a chance to answer because he was suddenly on the ground, blood pooling from somewhere. I screamed and knelt beside him, only to find my body lifted and jerked away, then black.

* * *

Hawk

"Daddy?"

"Hey, baby girl. Is everything okay?" I asked, pouring a cup of coffee in the compound kitchen.

"Hawk, I have your girls," the deep Russian voice came over the phone.

My body locked. "Who the fuck is this?"

"I will send demands in two hours. You contact the police or FBI, I will kill both of them."

The phone went dead.

"Fuck!" I bellowed. "Flea!"

Flea came running. "What's up, boss?"

"I want Booker and Mack here now. Some fuckhead has Payton and Lily. Get me a burner."

"On it," Flea said, and left the common room.

I headed toward Crow's office, pushing open the door and finding my president slamming the phone against the wall.

"Crow?"

"The Russians have Ash."

"Shit," I said. "They've got Payton and Lily."

"I've called an emergency lock down. Families are staying here for a few nights."

A knock at the door brought Flea with a burner. "Mack's here, Booker's five minutes out."

I nodded and dialed Brock.

"We know, Hawk," Brock said. "Team's movin'."

"We're movin' too, Brock."

"Don't think that's a good idea."

"Don't give a fuck."

"Try to keep it legal, Hawk," Brock warned.

"I'm doin' whatever it takes to get my girls."

Brock sighed. "I hear ya."

I hung up and headed to the common room.

* * *

Payton

I came to with a splitting headache and a dry mouth. I registered the sound of sniffling and opened my eyes, turning my head to find who was crying.

"Lily?" I rasped.

She sat up from her place on the dirty mattress. "Mama! I fought you wew dead."

"Come here, baby," I said, and held my arms out. They were secured with a zip tie, as were my ankles, but at least my hands were tied in front of me so I could hold her. I was grateful for small favors.

Lily, unbound, crawled into my lap and hugged me gently. "Awa you okay, Payton?"

"I'm fine, honey."

"Daddy's comin'."

"I know, baby girl."

I scanned the almost barren room. On the floor were two single mattresses and in the corner a bucket...I looked up...only one window too high to reach, then to my right, concrete stairs, which indicated we must be in a basement of sorts.

"Lily, can you touch my back and tell me if you feel anything?"

She patted me down and shook her head.

"Okay, baby. Thanks."

They found the gun. Not surprising, but I would have really liked a miracle right about now. I heard scuffling and pulled Lily closer as light appeared above us and a body was hurled down the stairs. If I didn't have Lily, I'm pretty sure I would have allowed my panic to overtake me. Lily whimpered and I gave her a gentle squeeze. "I've got you, honey, but let me check on this person, okay? Can you just sit on the mattress for a minute?"

She nodded and climbed off my lap and I shuffled to the woman, gently pulling the pillowcase off her head. She looked a little familiar to me, but I couldn't place her right away. She had a nasty bump on her head, but I was surprised she didn't have worse damage from the trip down the stairs.

"Fucking bastard," she hissed as she opened her eyes and let out a groan. "What the fuck?"

Her hands were tied behind her back, but her legs were free.

"Asswee," Lily said, and rushed to the woman's side.

"Hey, Lily," she said, and rolled in an attempt to sit up.

"Try not to move," I said. "I can't tell how bad you're hurt."

She frowned. "You're Hawk's woman. Payton, right?"

"Yes."

"I'm Ashley. Crow's daughter."

"Oh, right. I thought I recognized you." I frowned and helped her sit up. "How did you get messed up in this?"

"I suck at choosing men."

I bit my lip. "Oh."

"Hawk's gonna fuckin' rain down death."

"If he can find us," I whispered, low enough so Lily couldn't hear me.

"He'll find us."

I swallowed my fear and nodded.

"He will," Ashley said. "Trust me. Dad'll get him and Booker on it. No one can hide from them."

"My brother will help too."

"Oh, right. Isn't he FBI?"

I nodded. I was quickly figuring out the club knew a lot more about me than I knew about them.

Ashley shook her head. "Never thought I'd see a day where club and law business mixed. It's gonna be interesting."

"Why are you so calm?" I asked.

"Because we're still alive, my dad's a badass, and so is your old man. Until they hurt us, we have a chance to plan."

"Until?" I challenged.

"Well, let's be honest here, Payton, they're not good guys, so anything can happen."

"Great," I whispered.

"Will the bad guys huwt us, Mama?" Lily whispered.

I sent a look of warning toward Ashley, who didn't react. "We've got you, honey, and Daddy will come."

She nodded and crawled into my lap again.

Ashley made it to her feet and walked the space. "If we could find something sharp…something to cut our ties with, maybe we could fight our way out."

"Or maybe we could not risk our lives and wait."

She rolled her eyes as she continued to walk the space.

"Mama, I have to go potty," Lily whispered.

"Okay, honey." I swallowed down the bile at the sight of the bucket. "You'll need to use the bucket, honey."

I walked her through what she needed to do and, thank the Lord, she did it with no mess. Once we got out of here, I was going to buy the girl a freakin' pony.

Of course, now I had to pee. But I was determined to hold it for as long as I could.

The limited light we had coming through the window was disappearing faster than I would have liked.

"I found something," Ashley whispered.

"What?"

"There's a nail sticking out here…if you can use it to get loose, maybe you can get me loose."

"I think you've been watching too many movies," I

grumbled.

"Just try."

I shuffled to where she stood and found the nail she was referring to, but I knew from experience that zip ties were hard to break. Granted, I'd never been tied up, but had used them to keep cords organized in our entertainment unit and things like that. Neither Macey nor I could ever undo them without scissors or a really sharp knife.

Before I could do anything, however, we heard muffled popping and I knew it was gunfire. "Lily, come here," I demanded, and the three of us moved to the space behind the stairs. Ashley and I used our bodies to shield Lily, keeping her back to the wall.

The whole thing was over in minutes. I saw lights flickering from the stairs, then someone must have flipped a switch because light flooded into the room.

"Payton!" Hawk bellowed, his voice panicked.

"Here. We're here."

"Down here," Hawk called.

I shuffled us out of our hiding place and Lily and I were suddenly pinned in Hawk's arms.

"You came, Daddy."

"Yeah, baby girl. I'm here," he rasped.

Ashley was untied and pulled into a bear hug by her dad, before being ushered up the stairs.

"I can't move," I said, and Hawk released me. I gasped. "You're bleeding! Why are you bleeding? Cut me loose! I need to look."

"It's nothin', baby," he said, and lifted my face. "What the fuck did they do to you?"

"I think they just hit me. I was unconscious, but I'm okay."

Brock rushed down the stairs and pulled me into a hug. "You okay?"

"Yeah, I'm okay." *How many times did I have to say it?* "Can someone cut me loose please?"

Hawk pulled out a knife and did as I asked. I immediately pulled his cut away from his chest and lifted his shirt. "Honey, this doesn't look good."

"EMTs are here," Brock said. "Let's go."

The three of us were whisked into an ambulance and rushed to the emergency room. Alex's wound was much worse than he let on, and he required surgery and a two day stay at the hospital. Lily and I were fine, well, other than my minor concussion which meant I wasn't allowed to sleep for twenty-four hours. Kyle had been shot in the neck, but no arteries were hit, so after surgery, he made a full recovery.

Once again, my family closed ranks and Lily was cared for, I was fed ridiculous amounts of food…food solved everything in my mother's opinion…and Alex was fussed over. Once Alex was released from the hospital, he was set up in his room again, which meant we were never alone, and Alex was getting a little surly.

"Time for your pain meds," I said, and entered his room the day after he was released. He was standing at his bureau, pulling out a T-shirt. "What are you doing? You're supposed to be resting."

"I'm sick of being in bed, Payton," he said, and grimaced as he lifted his arms.

"Let me help."

Once his T-shirt was on, I checked his bandages and forced him to sit on the bed. He pulled me between his legs and kissed my stomach. "God, I want to fuck you so bad right now."

I chuckled. "Honey, you just had surgery. There will be none of that for at least two weeks. Doctor's orders."

"Fuckin' doctors," he hissed.

"If you promise to be really good, I might take care of you later."

His eyes brightened. "Yeah?"

"Yeah," I mimicked. "But this time it'll be you who can't move. Tearing your stitches is not an option."

He grinned. "I'm better at following the rules than you are."

I snorted. "Right. We'll go with that."

"Where's Lily?"

"She's upstairs. Brock and Bailey are here, so if you feel up to eating with us, dinner will be ready in about twenty minutes."

"Yeah, that'd be good, babe."

I smiled and kissed him. "Good. Lily's been asking if she can wake you."

"She can always wake me, baby."

"No she can't. But I love that you'd say that." I handed him the pain pills. "Take these and we'll head upstairs."

He did as he was told and we moved slowly up the stairs. I found it interesting that he straightened and suddenly got stronger as we entered the family room. His face was tight, but he forced a smile as he walked toward my family. I loved that he let his guard down with me, but wondered if he'd ever show anyone else his vulnerability. Probably not. I wrapped my arm around his waist gently and smiled up at him. As long as he was always honest with me, it was enough.

EPILOGUE

Payton

Eighteen months later…

I CAME AWAKE with a groan and Alex reached for my arm. Pain sliced through me and I whimpered.

"Payton?" he whispered.

"I think…ah…ooof."

Alex knifed off the bed and flooded the room with light.

"Too bright," I moaned.

He shut off the light again and turned on the bathroom one. "I'll get the bag. Should I call 9-1-1? I should get Lily. Should I get Lily, 'cause waking her might take time?"

I forced back a chuckle. "Call Mom, honey. I'm okay. You don't need to call 9-1-1."

He nodded and grabbed his cell phone. "Hey, Melissa? Yeah, she woke up in pain. Yeah. Ah…" He focused on me again. "How far apart are the contractions?"

"About six minutes," I said, and took a deep breath.

209

"Six minutes," Alex said. "Yes. Okay. Right. Thanks." He hung up and grabbed his jeans he'd dropped on the floor before we went to bed. "What do you need?"

"Well, if you can help me out of bed, honey, that would be a good start."

"Fuck, sorry." He rushed to my side and lifted me gently so I could stand. "Sweats. You want your sweats?"

"Yes, that would be great. Um, ohmigod," I breathed.

"What, baby?"

"I think my water just broke. I'm soaked."

"Okay. It's okay."

He helped me into clean clothes and guided me to the sofa at the end of our bed. As I sat attempting my breathing exercises, he finished dressing and then slid my fluffy slippers on my feet. Another contraction hit and I forced myself not to call out.

Alex knelt in front of me and took my hands. "You ready?"

I clamped my jaw shut and shook my head.

"Okay, we'll wait a minute."

We sat and waited through my contraction, my mother rushing into the room a few seconds after it passed.

"Hey, honey," she said, and cupped my face. "I can't believe my baby's having a baby."

I chuckled. "Me neither, Mom."

"Okay, Alex you get her to the hospital. I've got Lily and I called Macey. She's on her way. I'll join you as soon as Anna relieves me."

"Thanks," Alex said, and helped me stand.

We inched down the stairs and out to Alex's truck. He lifted me in, buckled my belt, and then we were off. We were less than ten minutes from the hospital, but it seemed to take longer, especially during contractions. Even with the pain, though, I was blissfully happy.

After the Russians had waged war on the club, the Dogs of Fire went on the offensive and took down several of the key players. I don't know how they did it and, quite frankly, I didn't want to know.

The final walk through of our house happened one week before our wedding which meant we had only a few days to move in, and this threw me into a stress tizzy, the likes no one had ever seen. Alex survived it, mostly because he drank a lot of beer. And I mean a *lot*. Even in the midst of what would be my final meltdown, I recognized the lengths he was going to make me happy (partly because my mother pointed them all out...yay, Mom). He organized every member of the club to act as moving men, which meant everything was moved in one day. Several of the club "old ladies" showed up to help me unpack, which added to my family, Macey, and Dani, so it made for light work.

Our wedding was perfect. My parents wanted a traditional Catholic wedding, which Alex didn't object to (much), but it was funny having biker men and women sitting in the beautiful cathedral in amongst my very formally dressed family and friends. It was perfect.

After a rockin' reception, Alex and I stayed one night at the Hotel Monaco in downtown Portland before we took off for a magical beach honeymoon in Cancun. My parents watched Lily (who I officially adopted), so we had an entire week to ourselves, and as promised, he'd packed some very creative toys including my clamps, which we utilized every night until I got pregnant. After that, I was just too sensitive.

Bailey discovered she was pregnant a month before I did, so we giddily planned the birth of our babies together. Kristen and Gordon had a beautiful baby boy who showed up a month early, and was now a perfect little walking terror. They couldn't have been happier.

Life for the James' family settled in to a surprisingly normal one for a badass biker bounty hunter and his elementary school teacher wife. I joked that I should write a book about our love story, considering it was just so unique.

Hunter Alexander James arrived six hours after my labor had begun, weighing in at seven pounds, eleven ounces and twenty-two inches long. He was healthy, he was beautiful, and he was all ours.

"You're so beautiful, baby," Alex whispered, and kissed me before kissing our son's head. Tears slid down his face as he smiled at us. "I'm in awe of you."

I ran my hand down his cheek and let my own tears flow. "Thank you for our life, Alex. Thank you for our children."

A tiny little gasp sounded and we looked to see Lily rushing into the room, my mom closely following. At six years old, Lily was beyond excited to be a big sister. She'd grown out of her speech issues, which honestly, I was kind of sad about, but I suppose I'd have to let my kids grow up at some point.

"Hey, honey," I said. "Meet your new brother."

Alex lifted Lily onto the bed and she stroked Hunter's hand. "He's so cute, Mommy."

"I know. Do you want to hold him?"

"Yes, please."

"Okay, come sit up here beside me and Daddy will help."

As the rest of my family piled into the room, Alex guided Hunter into Lily's loving and capable arms and I basked in the glow of unconditional love surrounding us. When Macey walked in to check on us, my circle was complete.

I had the best man in the world at my side, two gorgeous kids, plus the most loving friends and family on the planet.

Alex said that I'm his light, and perhaps I did help illuminate his road to a redemption of sorts. I'm not sure about all of that. What I do know, is that Alex is my protector, my lover, my soul mate, and my one true love, but most importantly, he is my awakening.

Piper Davenport is the alter-ego of *New York Times Bestselling Author*, Tracey Jane Jackson. She writes from a place of passion and intrigue, combining elements of romance and suspense with strong modern-day heroes and heroines.

She currently resides in the Pacific Northwest with her author husband, Jack Davenport, and an obnoxious YorkiePoo named Pepper who may or may not be an international spy.

Like Piper's FB page and get to know her!
(www.facebook.com/piperdavenport)

www.ingramcontent.com/pod-product-compliance
Lightning Source LLC
Chambersburg PA
CBHW060408310726
48976CB00003B/984